THE MONSTER OF SILVER CREEK

BY

BELINDA G. BUCHANAN

Cover photo by Bob Van Alphen

Chapter One

Nathan Sommers stared grimly at the photo of a young woman. Her body lay sprawled in the mud with her hands bound behind her. After a moment, his eyes moved on to the coroner's report.

"Chief?"

"What is it, Norma?"

Her face was serious. "We've got another one."

He kicked his chair back and got to his feet. "Where?"

"Graves Landing, near the point."

He hurried past her and out of the station.

Scrambling into his truck, he took off down Main Street with his lights flashing. He made a right and drove parallel with the lake for about a mile before turning down a narrow road. His stomach began to churn as he neared the point at Graves Landing.

There were several cars parked on either side— none of which, he noticed, were emergency response vehicles. Spotting his deputy's truck, he pulled off behind it and began the slow descent down the steep embankment.

"Morning, Chief."

"Jack," he said, ducking under the yellow tape. "Who found her?"

"A couple of hikers," he answered, leading him over to the body. "They were walking along the trail when they spotted her. I've taken their statement already."

Nathan took the pair of latex gloves he was holding out to him and solemnly knelt in front of the victim. Her long brown hair was matted in mud and leaves as she lay partially submerged in the silt. Dressed in navy shorts and a blood-stained tank top, her flawlessly tanned skin was in the process of turning a pale shade of gray. He saw the familiar marks on the left side of her chest just above the lining of her shirt. Her eyes were open and frozen in horror, revealing the absolute fear she had felt during the final moments of her life.

"Are you ready, Chief?" asked Jack, kneeling on the other side of her.

Nathan gave a short nod, noting that his deputy's complexion was nearly the same color as the girl's.

Leaning over, Jack slowly pulled the silver duct tape from her mouth, exposing her lips, which were parted and blue.

Nathan swallowed hard as he slipped his fingers inside her mouth. After a moment, they closed around a small solid object. He slowly pulled it out and turned the stone over in his palm. The number four was smeared on it.

"Go ahead and bag it," he said, handing it to his deputy. "Is she a local?"

"Don't know," Jack answered, taking the stone from him. "She didn't have any I.D. on her."

As Nathan shifted his weight to his other foot, he caught sight of something shiny reflecting in the girl's hair. A closer look revealed it to be a gold necklace. The clasp was intact, but the delicate chain attached to it had been broken in half. Picking it up, he studied the charm that dangled from its end.

"It's the Star of David," Jack said quietly.

Nathan handed it to him to bag and stood up. "Is the coroner on his way?"

"No, he's got two women in the final stages of labor. His office said he would be over here as soon as he could."

Nathan stripped off his gloves and surveyed the scene. The body was partially hidden in some loose brush near the edge of the walking trail. This part of the path was more secluded and normally didn't see a lot of traffic. To the right of the trail was the lake, which ran parallel with it for two miles, all the way around the point, before ending at the cabins. The other side contained nothing but a steep slope that led up to the road.

Jack pointed at the footprints along the ground. "Those are from our hikers."

Nathan looked at the impressions. Two sets of prints strayed off the trail and came close to the body.

A burst of static sounded. "Collins, do you read?"

Jack grabbed the radio mic on his epaulet. "Go ahead."

"We've got a boating accident over at the north side by the old ramp. No injuries reported."

"I'll take it," Nathan said.

"10-4, Norma. The chief is responding."

As he turned to go, he noticed that a rather large crowd of onlookers had gathered at the top of the embankment. Nathan studied their faces one by one for a moment. "Bag anything that looks suspicious."

Collins nodded as he snapped a picture of the victim. "I'll show her photo around. See if anyone recognizes her."

As Nathan began making his way up the slope, he was inundated with questions.

"What happened to her, Chief?"

"Can't say," he replied curtly.

"I heard she's got the marks on her just like the others. Is that right?"

"Are they fang marks?"

"Who was she?"

The crowd continued to badger him as he climbed into the seat of his truck and reached to close the door.

Mac Hodges suddenly appeared. "What do you think, Chief?" he said, holding on to the door. "Is it just like the others?"

Nathan clenched his jaw. Mac's breath smelled of cigarettes and coffee, which together gave off an aroma of cow manure.

"Is that number four?"

"Can't say." Nathan jerked the door shut and headed down the road to where the accident was.

Chapter Two

Nathan stood near the water's edge talking to the driver of the Jet Ski. "Have you been drinking any alcohol today, sir?"

The guy squinted up at him as he shook his head. "No, sir."

"No?" Nathan turned behind him and looked up the boat ramp. The handlebars of a Jet Ski lay on the ground beneath a giant elm tree. The rest of the craft sat lodged in its branches ten feet up.

He folded his arms across his tattoo-covered chest and shrugged. "I just wasn't watching where I was going."

"*Hey!* What the *hell* have you done to my Jet Ski?"

Nathan glanced to his right and saw Sam Bryant heading towards them.

Bryant got right in the boy's face and tapped him on the chest. "What the *hell* happened?"

"Hey, man! *Back off!*" he said, putting his hands out to his sides.

Nathan stepped between them. "All right, Sam. Let's just calm down."

"It's the same *damn* thing every year, Chief. These jerks come here from up north and think that they own the freakin' lake!"

"Why don't you stop renting to them, then?" he asked pointedly.

The scowl on Bryant's face was quickly replaced with a sheepish grin, reminding Nathan of a Cheshire cat.

"Do you know how much money an hour I make for these things?"

Nathan's mouth twitched. "File a claim. You can pick up a copy of the accident report later in the week."

"All right," Bryant said, letting out an exasperated sigh.

Nathan took the driver by his arm. "Come with me."

"Where are we going?"

"I'm going to need you to take a Breathalyzer test."

He planted his feet and pulled back. "Come on, man! How about if I pay for the Jet Ski, instead?"

Nathan shook his head as he led him up the algae-covered boat ramp. "Sorry."

"Hey, Chief?"

"Yeah?"

"How am I supposed to get that thing out of the tree?"

He looked over his shoulder. "Beats me."

"You're not much help, you know."

"I've gotta go, Sam. I'll catch up with you later."

"Yeah, I heard about the girl. Is she another victim?"

Nathan kept walking, pretending he hadn't heard him.

~

Nathan hurried up the steps to the police station and through the door. The reading from the Breathalyzer had shown that the driver of the Jet Ski was not legally drunk, but it was enough to place him under arrest.

"Oh, Chief, I'm glad you're back," Norma said, following him into his office.

He turned slightly. Norma was a rather large woman but made absolutely no sound when she walked. She always just seemed to appear behind him like an apparition.

She had several slips of paper in her hands. "Beadie Johnson swears there's a peeping Tom outside her house and wants you to come by."

He unclipped his Glock from his belt and put it in the top drawer of his desk as he listened to her go on.

"There's a lady that called and said her neighbor's dog killed her cat. And the traffic light is out on Harmony and Fifth." Her plump face smiled sweetly at him as she handed him the messages.

He leaned back in his chair for a moment. "Where are our four-way stop signs?"

"Behind the building in the storage shed."

"All right," he said, rubbing the back of his neck. "I'll get the signs set up and then go see the cat lady. Tell Mrs. Johnson I'll stop by later on today."

~

Nathan double-checked the address Norma had given him. It was for the old Anderson house which he knew had been vacant for the past year. He started to radio her but as he pulled into the driveway, he noticed that the garage door was raised and had several cardboard boxes sitting inside it.

Glancing to his right, he could see a young woman standing on the front porch wiping her eyes, while an older man waited on the lawn a few feet away.

A German shepherd, tethered on a leash, began to furiously wag its tail as Nathan made his way over.

Upon seeing him, the man scrambled to meet him halfway. "Chief? My name's Nick Donaldson."

It was obvious to Nathan that he wanted to tell his side of the story first. "Wait just a minute, okay?" he said, holding up his hand.

Mr. Donaldson hesitated for a moment, and then reluctantly stepped aside.

Nathan turned his attention to the woman. "Ma'am? I'm Chief Sommers."

"Katie Winstead," she answered tearfully.

He couldn't help noticing how pretty she was, even though her face was streaked with tears. "Can you tell me what happened?" he asked, taking out his notepad.

"Yes," she said quietly. "That man's *dog* killed my cat for absolutely no reason! He just attacked her and shook her like a rag doll!"

Nathan stopped writing and looked up as her voice suddenly changed into that of a billowing dragon.

"He should be put down for what he did!" she continued.

Nathan noticed the light blue towel lying on the porch just behind her feet. A red stain seeped through the top of it. Stepping forward, he knelt down to take a look. A small yellow paw fell out from underneath it as he lifted the cover.

This sent the woman into a spasm of sobs.

Mr. Donaldson tapped him on his shoulder. "Chief Sommers?"

He let the towel drop back on the cat and stood up.

"I've already explained to this lady that it was an accident. Bo didn't know any better. I mean he's a dog. It was a cat. That's what they do." He looked helplessly at Nathan. "Bo has always come over here to do his business because, you know," he said, shrugging, "no one has lived here for a while. When she moved in the other day, I didn't know she had a cat."

Nathan studied the dog for a moment. Bo was sitting beside his master's leg with his tongue hanging out of the side of his mouth. He seemed to be quite pleased with himself.

He gave Donaldson a nod. "From now on, keep him on your own property unless he's on a leash, all right?"

"Yes, sir." He turned towards his neighbor and gave her a humble look. "Miss, I'm really, really sorry. I hope you can forgive me and my dog."

She glared at him to such a degree that Nathan felt the man was going to burst into flames any second now.

"Come on, boy." Mr. Donaldson led the dog across the lawn and around to his own backyard.

The woman abruptly shifted her gaze to Nathan. "You're not going to do anything about what that monster did to my cat?"

"I'm sorry," he said, shaking his head, "but it was an accident." And quite frankly, he had bigger monsters at the moment to concern himself with.

Her cheeks darkened as something that resembled lightning shot out of her eyes. "Well, that's just great!"

Nathan gestured at the towel. "Would you like me to take the cat away for you?"

His words were met with an icy silence.

"If you want, I can bury him for you—"

She turned on her heel and went through the front door, slamming it behind her.

"*Or not,*" he said with a sigh.

~

Nathan wiped the sweat from his forehead as he walked up the steps to the station house. They were just barely into June and the temperatures had already climbed into the nineties.

Norma was waiting for him as he came through the door. "Collins radioed in and said they found the victim's purse. Her name's Missy Rosenberg. She lives over in Wibaux County."

"Did you get hold of her family?"

She nodded and handed him a slip of paper. "Her mother's on her way over."

Shit. Nathan crumpled the paper between his fingers. "Where's the body now?"

"The morgue, why —"

"Go ahead and arrange for Harry to do the autopsy now."

"But you know he won't do it unless the next of kin's been notified first."

He shook his head impatiently. "Norma, I need you to do this for me right now. Before the mother comes. Understand?"

Norma's pencil-drawn eyebrows crinkled up as she looked at him. She liked Nathan but didn't like the fact that sometimes he avoided protocol. "All right," she said after a moment.

"Thank you," he said softly. "Tell him I'm on my way over."

Chapter Three

Dr. Jensen leaned over Missy Rosenberg's body, carefully examining the wounds on her chest.

Nathan stood in the far corner of the room, silently watching. The girl's skin had turned a pasty green and was now filleted like a fish. He crossed his arms and swallowed hard, trying to keep the gag from coming up.

The doctor gave him a curious glance. "Do you want to come closer to see?"

"No, I'm fine where I'm at."

He seemed to be smiling through his mask as he put the calipers away. "Well, it looks to be the same cause of death as the other three. Whatever he used, punctured the aorta. She died within two minutes."

"Any skin or hair under her fingernails?" Nathan asked, hoping against hope that the killer had made a mistake this time.

"No, she's clean," Jensen said, stripping off his gloves. "There was no evidence of forced intercourse either. The only other marks I found on her were where her wrists were bound." He held up the plastic bag with the stone in it. "The writing on it *is* blood...I'm sure the test will confirm it's the victim's."

"How soon will you have the results?"

Jensen tilted his head. "You know, Nathan, I do have live patients to attend to."

Nathan sighed inwardly. Besides serving as Silver Creek's coroner for the past twenty years, Jensen was also the town's beloved obstetrician. The two jobs rarely interfered with one another, but when they did, he made it clear where his priorities lay. "I know you're busy, Harry," he said after a moment. "But this is really important."

The doctor pushed his glasses up, letting them rest on top of his head. "I'll put a rush on it."

Nathan nodded in appreciation. Despite all his bellyaching, Jensen was extremely good at his job. "Any guess on what he used to kill her?"

"No, I've never seen anything like it. But I *can* tell you that he used a lot of force. It went right through her aorta, nearly severing it."

A nurse in scrubs poked her head through the swinging door. "Excuse me. The victim's mother is here to identify the body."

Nathan suddenly cast his gaze upon the floor.

Dr. Jensen pursed his lips. "Give me two minutes, Jean."

The nurse nodded and disappeared.

"*Goddamn it,* Nathan! You said you wouldn't do that to me again!"

"I'm sorry, Harry, but she was Jewish. I was afraid her mother would've stood in the way. I'd rather beg for forgiveness."

"Well, that's just great for *you*," he said, grabbing a sterile sheet, "but I'm always the one left holding the bag! This girl's mother is coming in to see her daughter, and she's lying here cut open and dressed like a *deer!*"

"I'm sorry," he said, moving past him and out the door.

"I seriously doubt that," Jensen grumbled.

Nathan made his way across the waiting room and stopped at the counter, which was vacated at the moment. As he waited for the nurse to return, he noticed a small woman with short brown hair sitting in one of the chairs that lined the wall. Her hands were clasped tightly together as she stared at the floor.

"Did you get everything you needed, Chief?"

The woman suddenly looked up, locking eyes with him.

He quickly shifted his attention to Jean, who was now standing behind the counter. "Yes, thanks."

The woman watched him as he leaned over the desk and said something to the nurse in a low voice.

The nurse involuntarily glanced at her and then nodded.

Nathan made his way up the stairs and to the exit. Before his hands touched the door he could hear the woman's wails.

Chapter Four

"Need anything else, Chief?" the waitress asked, sliding his burger and fries in front of him.

"I'm good, thanks," he answered loud enough to be heard over the chatter. Even though it was late in the afternoon, the small diner was packed.

"All right," she said, leaving the bill face down on the counter.

Nathan glanced at the crowd around him. Most, if not all of them, were vacationers. From May through September people from all over flocked to Silver Creek. The town sat nestled right in the middle of Prairie County and held the distinct title of being the largest lake in the tristate area, boasting nearly three hundred miles of shoreline.

As he began salting his fries, he found himself wishing for October. He longed for the peace and quiet that the first frost always brought.

"Hey, Nathan," Collins said as he took the stool next to him.

"Jack."

"Did you learn anything new from Jensen?"

"Nothing that we didn't already know from the others."

Jack rubbed his forehead and sighed. "I don't like this, Nathan. This guy is killing people right under our —"

"I know," he answered, cutting him off.

His deputy gave him a bewildered look.

Nathan gestured with his eyes. "There are too many ears here."

Jack glanced around the room as if noticing the crowd of people for the very first time. "Sorry."

"It's all right," Nathan said, feeling his frustration.

The waitress came over and pulled a pad from the front of her apron. "Hey, Jack. What can I get for you?"

"Same as the chief."

"Sure thing," she said, slipping her pen back over her ear. "Congratulations, by the way. I hear you and Cheryl are having a girl."

He suddenly broke into a broad grin. "Yep."

"I'll get your order right out."

Jack's smile faded as quickly as it had come when he caught Nathan's gaze.

"A girl, huh? That's great, Jack."

He gave him an awkward nod and looked away. "Yeah."

The clinking of plates and glasses overtook the restaurant as an uneasy silence surrounded them.

~

Mrs. Rosenberg's fingers trembled as she took the Styrofoam cup from Nathan.

He closed the door to the interrogation room, which also served as the employee break room, and sat down across from her. He placed his hands flat on the metal table and drew a deep breath. "Mrs. Rosenberg, I'm very sorry about your daughter."

She gave him a nod, seemingly too distraught to speak at the moment.

A young woman, who had accompanied her to the station, reached over and squeezed her forearm. "I'm Missy's friend, Tiffany," she explained when she noticed him staring at her.

Nathan pulled a pen from his shirt pocket. "Can either of you tell me why Missy was in Silver Creek?"

Tiffany's eyes immediately began to water. "Missy and I came up here two days ago. We were renting a cabin on the lake..." Her voice trailed off as the reality of the whole situation began to sink in.

"When was the last time you saw or spoke with her?"

"About three o'clock yesterday."

"What were you doing?"

She gave him a slight shrug. "We were on the beach, just hanging around. Then I met this guy, and he asked me to go jet skiing with him." Tears began to roll down her cheeks. "I didn't want to leave her by herself, but Missy told me to go on. She said that she would meet me back at the cabin around six. We'd made plans to have dinner at *The Sea Shack.*"

"And did you?"

"No," she replied, wiping her eyes. "When I got back to the cabin she wasn't there. About an hour later, she texted me saying she'd met a guy and told me not to wait up for her."

He made some notes on the legal pad in front of him before continuing. "Did you find that odd?"

"No," she said definitively. "I was happy for her. She'd been so sad lately. I was glad that she'd met someone."

"Why was she sad?"

"She had just broken up with her fiancé," Mrs. Rosenberg spoke quietly.

Nathan looked over at her, having forgotten that she was in the room.

"Missy was completely devastated. I remember being happy when she told me she was coming here with Tiffany. I thought the sun might do her some good."

He reached behind him for a box of tissues and placed it in front of her. "Did she say anything else to you about this guy she'd met?" he asked, directing his question at Tiffany. "Anything at all?"

"No, nothing."

"What did you do before going to the beach?"

"We slept in because—" She stopped and gave Missy's mother an apologetic look. "We were both a little hungover. After we'd gotten ready, we went over to the boardwalk. We had some lunch, bought some souvenirs...stuff like that."

"During the time you were together, did you ever see anybody watching you, or following you?"

"No, not that I was aware of," she replied, seeming startled by his question. "I mean, the beach was full of people yesterday. Even if someone *had* been, I doubt if we would have noticed."

He slid the pad over to her. "I need for you to write down the name and number of Missy's fiancé. And I'll need your keys to the cabin."

Mrs. Rosenberg's breath jerked out of her. "Chief Sommers?"

"Yes?" he said, forcing himself to look at her.

"When can we take my daughter's body home? I want to bury her as soon as possible."

"The coroner has signed off on the release form, so you can make the arrangements today if you wish."

She suddenly stood up and grabbed her purse.

Nathan pushed his chair back and got to his feet. "Ma'am, if there's anything I can do, please don't hesitate to ask."

"I think you've done enough," she said, giving him a cold look. "You've already seen to it that her body was desecrated."

~

Nathan sat in his office staring at the contents of Missy's purse. Everything lay spread out in front of him as he went over each of the items. Inside her billfold, he found two folded receipts. One was for an ATM withdrawal made yesterday morning at ten-thirty for fifty dollars. The other was for some merchandise purchased on the boardwalk. He counted the bills and saw that she had around thirty-five dollars left. It appeared that her credit cards were still intact.

He picked up her Blackberry and began scrolling through her pictures. The most recent one was of her standing on the beach near the water's edge. The angle of the photo was slightly tilted, indicating to him that it was a selfie. This was the last photo taken of her before she died. The last footprint she had left upon this earth — yet it led to nowhere.

Grazing over the screen with his thumb, he quickly checked her outgoing calls. Over the past three days, she had phoned her mother twice, with the last call being made around eleven o'clock.

A further check of her voice mail revealed she had not received any recent messages, but she had sent a text to Tiffany around seven-thirty last night. It read, *'T met a QT so dwu4me. M'.*

"Goodnight, Chief," Norma called to him.

"See you in the morning," he said absently as he stared at the words. "Norma, wait." He pushed his chair back and ran out of his office.

She stopped and looked at him expectantly.

"What does this mean?" He held the Blackberry up for her to see.

She fingered her reading glasses that hung from a chain around her neck and peered down at the small screen. Her nose crinkled as she squinted. "Met a cutie...don't wait up for me."

Nathan scratched the side of his head as he turned the phone back around.

"You know, Chief," Norma said, arching an eyebrow, "you really need to get out more."

Chapter Five

It was well after nine by the time Nathan finally arrived home that evening. He laid his gun down on the table beside him and sat down wearily in the brown leather recliner. He let his head rest against the back of it and closed his eyes, trying to shut out the day. But Missy Rosenberg's face, as well as the cries from her mother, still lingered in his mind, making it impossible to do so.

A bitter sigh fell from his lips as his eyes snapped open. During his years spent as a homicide detective, he'd always felt that it was his job to bring justice for the dead. Putting the killer behind bars gave him a sense of satisfaction that he was bringing closure to their loved ones.

Over the last few weeks, however, he'd slowly begun to realize just how wrong he was. For when darkness fell at the end of the day, those that had fallen prey to evil would still be dead…and their families would still be grieving for them.

He slowly sat forward and leaned over to untie his work boots. As he did, his wedding picture caught his eye, just like it had every night for the past two years. He kicked off his boots and picked up the silver frame.

He let his fingers trace over Jenny's face, all the while wishing he could feel her skin. There were times that he could almost capture it. It was always there, but just out of his reach.

Nathan's emotions began to churn, causing him to set the frame down. Wanting to avoid the impending tears, he quickly moved his attention to the case files in his lap.

One by one, he opened up the folders and laid them out meticulously on the coffee table in front of him. His eyes were immediately drawn to the first victim. Carol Fuqua was a bank teller who had worked right across the street from the station house. Well-known and well-liked, her death had sent shockwaves of terror across this close-knit community.

He began sifting through the photos that had been taken at the crime scene, hoping to find something that he'd missed. The images he'd come to know by heart reflected back at him, yet revealed nothing new. By the time he got to the last picture, his jaw had grown rigid. Carol's hands had been bound behind her so tightly that the duct tape had left deep lacerations in her wrists.

No longer wishing to view them, he flipped the photos over and concentrated on reading through his notes. Her father had placed a frantic call to the police when she hadn't come home from work the night of May eleventh. While a routine search had turned up nothing, the next afternoon Carol's car had been found on a rural road near Graves Landing. The keys were still in the ignition, but they, along with the rest of the vehicle, had been wiped clean of fingerprints. Two days later, a fisherman had found her body in some tall brush by the water's edge.

Nathan had spent the next few days interviewing everyone that knew Carol on a personal level, and even though they were all as shocked as he was to learn of her violent death, none of them seemed to know anything. The information her father had provided was vague. He thought she had a prepaid cell phone but a search of her car hadn't turned one up.

He solemnly closed the file and rubbed the back of his neck before moving on to the next one. As the minutes ticked away, the frustration inside of him began to grow. Four women, all of them young and pretty, had been found murdered around the lake, but the similarities stopped after that. Carol was a local, while the others were from neighboring counties. Their hair types weren't even the same.

The killer had left no fingerprints, no hairs, no fibers—no clues of any kind behind. And the murder weapon itself was just as perplexing. It caused two small wounds over the heart, sometimes rupturing the aorta, but always puncturing it. The openings were relatively small in diameter and evenly spaced three inches apart.

He studied the photo of the stone that had been found inside the mouth of the third victim, a twenty-eight-year-old teacher from Wibaux County. Dr. Jensen confirmed that it had been placed there post-mortem. This was the same conclusion on all the women. The rocks were small, round, and smooth to the touch. Unfortunately, there wasn't anything unique about them as they could be found anywhere along the shoreline.

The minutes turned into hours for Nathan, and it was after midnight before he fell into bed. But even as darkness surrounded him, he found that his mind was still processing the cases, refusing to let him sleep. There were so many unanswered questions. Was the killer a local, or just passing through? Did he like to stand around and watch the police? Had he been watching them this morning?

He slipped his hands behind his head and stared at the ceiling fan as it slowly turned above him. He wished that he had at least one piece of concrete evidence. Just something that would point him in the right direction.

After a moment, he turned over on his side and forced his eyes to close. His hand instinctively moved along the mattress in search of Jenny. She, of course, wasn't there, nor would she ever be there again. His throat began to ache as her loss washed over him again for the thousandth time.

Chapter Six

"Can I get you some coffee, Chief Sommers?" The mayor's aide offered him a courteous smile as she showed him in.

"No, I'm good. Thanks, Erin."

"He should be here momentarily," she said, walking towards the door.

He couldn't help noticing that her perfume lingered for far too long after she had gone. He checked his watch before letting his eyes wander around the mayor's spacious office. Filled with expensive knick-knacks and handmade cherry furniture, it was no comparison to the prefabricated desks and folding tables that decorated the station house.

His feet sank into the plush carpeting as he walked over to one of the windows. Crystal Park sat directly across the street, giving him a bird's-eye view. It was impressive, to say the least, and Nathan probably would have allowed himself to enjoy it if not for the fact that four girls had been murdered in the city he'd been sworn to protect. Feeling his anxiousness returning, he moved away from the glass.

Several mounted fish, two of which had been caught at Silver Creek, adorned the walls. The mayor was an avid fisherman and Nathan had heard the stories of how he had landed each and every one several times over.

He shifted his gaze to the eight-foot blue marlin that hung behind his desk. It was the mayor's pride and joy, and it was so big that it just barely fit between the windows. The cobalt blue on the fish's back shimmered brightly against the warm beige paint of the walls. The mayor had caught it off the southern tip of Florida during a fishing expedition a few years ago. Nathan shook his head, realizing that he could almost recite the story by heart.

A large aerial portrait of the lake was fixed above the conference table on the far side of the room. It was an old photo, having been taken nearly forty years ago. Nathan had always liked the picture. It reflected the natural beauty the lake once held. There was only one road leading to it from the town, and the only objects surrounding it were the trees.

Today, the north side of the lake held over fifty cabins. More than twenty acres of forest had been eradicated in order to make room for them.

Silver Creek Lake had been upgraded in the late seventies, as this small, struggling town recognized the potential revenue it could bring. Countless tons of white sand had been brought in to make the shoreline. It wasn't long before the town was on the map.

"Sorry to keep you waiting, Nathan."

He turned from the picture and nodded. "Good morning, Tom."

The mayor looked at him and sighed before taking the seat behind his desk. "This is a *hell* of a way to kick off the summer."

Nathan bit his tongue as he sat down across from him. When it came to his chief of police, the mayor was all business.

Tom Manning's stern gaze went from him to the photo that graced the top of his desk.

Nathan shifted uncomfortably in his chair. Although he couldn't see the picture, he knew it was of Jenny.

"I need an update on the situation." Manning took off his glasses and began polishing them with the wide end of his necktie.

"The fourth victim was from Wibaux. The mother identified the body yesterday —"

"I don't care about any of that," he said, waving his hand as if the information was irrelevant. "Do you have any leads? Any clues?"

Nathan hesitated. "No."

Manning stood up and marched over to the portrait of the lake. "These killings have to stop." He tapped his index finger against the middle of the photo. "*This* is our bread and butter. We *live* for the summers. And the people deserve the right to come here and enjoy themselves without the risk of being murdered. I just came from a meeting with the Chamber of Commerce and they told me that tourism is down nearly thirty percent for the season."

Nathan got to his feet and went to stand on the other side of the picture. "I've got my men knocking on every cabin. We're stopping every tourist and asking them if they've seen or heard anything."

"What about the FBI? Are they coming?"

"They're sending me a profiler. He's supposed to be here today."

"That's it?"

Nathan folded his arms across his chest. "That's all they're willing to do at the moment."

The muscle in Manning's jaw twitched as he shook his head. "From now on, I want a daily update."

Nathan stifled a sigh as he turned to leave. "Yes, sir."

"Sommers?"

He stopped and looked over his shoulder.

"You *know* that this is an election year."

Nathan nodded, surprised that it had taken him this long to remind him.

The mayor looked back at the photo. "We'll *both* be out of a job if you don't put an end to this soon."

~

Nathan met Jack on the steps outside the station house. "Where are you headed?" he asked, stepping out of his way.

"I've got to get to court," he called over his shoulder. "You know that Hemmings always rules against us if we're late."

Nathan pursed his lips. Judge Hemmings was a crotchety old fart who thought that the sun rose and set with him.

"By the way, that profiler from the FBI is here. I gave him the files and put him in the interrogation room."

A slight sense of relief came over Nathan. Maybe now they would have something to go on. "Thanks."

"I'll see you later."

As he watched Jack hurry down the sidewalk, he caught sight of someone faintly familiar coming towards him. It was the cat lady from yesterday. Unfortunately, she was too close for him to duck inside and pretend that he hadn't seen her. As she drew near, he gave her an awkward nod. "Ma'am."

"Chief Sommers," she replied curtly.

He opened his mouth to say something else, but she had already gone past. He leaned against the rail and sighed as he watched her cross the street. Her tiny arms swung deliberately back and forth in a no-nonsense manner before disappearing inside the bakery.

～

Nathan rested his shoulder against the trunk of a large tree as he watched Mr. Horner squatting down beside the edge of the hiking trail. For the past five minutes, he had done nothing but stare at the ground.

Horner slid the photo of Missy Rosenberg out of the folder and began combing his mustache with his finger. "The coroner confirmed that there was no sign of forced intercourse?"

"That's correct," Nathan said. "The guy could've used a condom, but there was no obvious bruising or tearing—along with the fact that she was found fully clothed."

He tapped his pen against the pad of paper. "Interesting."

"Why's that?"

Horner held the notepad on his knee as he jotted something down.

Nathan waited for his answer but got nothing. He crossed his arms, trying to hide his irritation. The profiler had asked him to see the place where Missy Rosenberg's body had been found. They had been here for over an hour now, but the man had yet to give him anything of value.

"Chief?"

He reached for his walkie-talkie. "Go ahead, Norma."

"Can you respond to a possible 273-D?"

Horner looked over at him. "Go ahead. I'll be another hour here at least."

He held the radio to his lips as he headed up the embankment. "I'm on my way. What's the address?"

~

Nathan could hear the yelling as he hurried up the flight of steps towards apartment 519. "Police! Open up!" he said, banging against the door.

The screaming suddenly stopped.

A few moments later, a tall, stocky man with dark-brown eyes appeared at the door. "Yeah?"

"Everything okay?" Nathan asked, putting his boot against the door so the man couldn't close it.

"We were just havin' a little argument," he explained with a shrug. "You know how it is."

Nathan pushed the door back with his hand and saw a woman sitting on the couch. A toddler with brown curly hair clung to her chest as pieces of a lamp lay shattered on the floor beside them.

He returned his attention to the man standing in front of him. "Sir, I'm going to need you to step outside for just a minute."

The man puffed up his chest and took a small, but threatening advance towards him. "Why? This is *my* place. You can't ask me to leave."

Nathan subtly moved his hand to his weapon. He knew from experience how quickly domestic disputes could escalate. "I'm not asking you to leave, sir. I'm asking you to wait outside for a moment." His voice was calm but carried authority.

The man suddenly glanced over his shoulder.

Before Nathan could do anything, he had already locked eyes with the woman.

"I'll be right outside," he said to her in a low voice.

Nathan swung the door closed behind him and went to kneel in front of the woman. "Ma'am? I'm Chief Sommers."

She met his words with a stone-cold stare.

Deciding to try a different approach, he reached up and gently touched the little girl's hand. "What's your daughter's name?"

The little girl, who looked to be about two, immediately recoiled.

"Did your husband hurt you or your daughter?" he asked, lowering his hand.

"He's my boyfriend."

"What's your name?"

"Shauna White."

"Did he hit you?" he asked, taking note of the red mark on the right side of her cheek.

"No. We just had an argument." As she spoke, her tongue fell through the hole where one of her front teeth used to be.

"What about?"

"It doesn't matter," she said, shaking her head. "We're fine."

Nathan could see old bruises peeking out from underneath the sleeve of her shirt. "Did he give you those?"

"No."

He stood up and reached into his back pocket for his wallet. "This is the phone number for a shelter you can go to."

The woman hesitated, and then took the card from him.

"I can drive you there now if you like."

She closed her fist around it and began crumpling it between her fingers. When she was done, she tossed it on the floor at his feet.

A sigh fell from his lips as he turned away.

When Nathan stepped outside, the man was leaning against the wall, smoking a cigarette.

"What'd she tell you?"

"She didn't tell me anything. What's your name?"

"Miguel Flores," he said, blowing the smoke in his direction.

There were a lot of things that Nathan could have said to him at this point, but he felt it would have dire consequences for the woman. "Try and keep the yelling to a minimum," he said, making his way down the corridor.

A middle-aged man stood waiting for him as he neared the exit. "Thank you for coming."

"Are you the one that called?"

"Yes. I'm the landlord."

He couldn't help noticing how the man held his hands. They were pressed together, knuckle touching knuckle, but not interlocked. His eyes flitted in every direction but his. He reminded Nathan of a squirrel scurrying for nuts.

"I've had nothing but trouble with them since they moved in."

"What kind of trouble?"

"*This* kind. They're also three months behind on the rent. One of your deputies served them with an eviction notice a couple of weeks ago."

~

Nathan pushed a small red thumbtack into the map on his office wall. He had to push hard to get it to go through the paneling. There were four blue tacks spread a few centimeters apart around a body of water. The red tacks were put in the areas of Wibaux and McCone counties where three of the victims lived. A single yellow tack was pinned in the area of Hollow Lane where Carol, the first victim, resided.

He put his hands on his waist and looked at the radius. All of the killings were within two miles of each other. But the victims lived hundreds of miles apart. The link was the lake. To him, that meant that the killer was a local.

He suppressed a yawn as he rubbed the back of his neck. It had been a long day, and he wanted nothing more than to go home and take a hot shower. Unfortunately, he had no idea when that would be.

"You need anything before I take off?" asked Jack, poking his head inside the doorway.

He turned from the map. "No. Have a good evening."

Jack nodded at the interrogation room. "Is he still in there?"

"Yeah," Nathan replied, walking around to his desk. "How was court?"

"Hemmings ruled in our favor for seven out of nine cases, but threw three out," he said, pressing his shoulder against the doorjamb.

Nathan leaned back in his chair and clasped his hands behind his head. "That's an improvement, I guess," he answered, trying not to sigh.

"Do you want to come over early on Sunday before dinner and watch the game?"

He gave his deputy a nod. "Yeah. I'll bring the beer."

The sound of footsteps made Jack turn to look. Horner was heading their way. "I'll talk to you tomorrow."

"Goodnight, Jack."

He stepped aside allowing him to come in.

"Thank you for waiting, Chief Sommers."

"No problem," he said, getting to his feet.

Horner closed the door behind him. "I'm going to dispense with the pleasantries and just get right down to it if you don't mind."

"That's fine," Nathan replied, being only too happy to oblige. "So what can you tell me about our killer?"

"Based on the information I've gathered," he began, perching himself on the edge of the desk. "I've come up with what I believe to be the physical traits the killer possesses."

"Such as?"

Horner slipped on his reading glasses and glanced down at his notes. "The person you are looking for is definitely a male, probably six feet or taller, and is predominately left-handed."

"How do you know he's left-handed?"

He pulled a photo from one of the files. "This is a picture of the duct tape that was used to restrain Missy Rosenberg."

Nathan recognized the picture. Dr. Jensen had taken it after removing the tape from her wrists.

"Do you see the tear pattern?" Horner pointed to the edge. "It's a clean tear until you get to the very end — then it curves slightly to the right. This tells me two things. Number one: since no saliva was found on it, he didn't tear it with his teeth. He used his fingers. Number two: a person that is predominantly left-handed will hold a roll of tape in his right hand and tear it with their left. The result is a curve to the right. A right-handed person will do just the opposite, causing it to curve left. When the killer bound the victims' hands, he unrolled it left, then over and under. That's also a left-handed trait."

"Were the ligature marks the same on all four victims?"

Horner nodded as he stuck the photo back in the file.

Nathan folded his arms. Although that information was interesting, he didn't find it to be very useful. It wasn't as if he could go out and arrest someone just because they were left-handed. "What else can you tell me?"

"He has an obsession with fear — or I should say — an obsession with his *victims'* fear. He gets off on it." Horner let his glasses fall against his chest. "That's why he kills. Based on the severity of the ligature marks, those women were bound for hours. Their last moments of life, when they know they are going to die...he revels in it. He *savors* it. It's what drives him to kill. That's why he doesn't sexually assault them. He doesn't need to. He probably feels a rush of adrenaline or a burst of euphoria that no drug can come close to matching."

Nathan rubbed his eyes trying to take in everything he had just told him. "Do you know why he targeted these specific women?"

"He probably picked them because they looked vulnerable. These were all small women, probably defenseless. He likes to execute power and control over them; it helps to validate his self-worth."

Nathan watched as he began flipping through the photos.

"I also strongly believe he killed all of his victims somewhere else before dumping their bodies."

"Why do you think that?"

Horner scratched his mustache for a moment. "When an aorta is punctured from the outside, there's going to be a lot of blood. With these women, the only traces found were on their clothing. There should have been some on the ground."

"Any thoughts on the weapon he used?"

"I have no idea on that. I'm sorry. *But* he knows *how* to use it, and knows exactly *where* to use it. There is no hesitation in him when he kills. He uses brute force." He paused to shake his head. "And he *doesn't* feel remorse."

"Are we dealing with a psychopath?"

"Not necessarily." Horner placed the files on Nathan's desk and clasped his hands together. "The guy's smart. But not smart enough to avoid attention."

"What do you mean?"

"The stones. They're his signature. He's evoking fear into the local law enforcement, as well as the public, by using shock and awe. That in itself may be his undoing. I think eventually he *will* slip up—make a mistake." He checked his watch and got to his feet. "I've written a detailed report for you," he said, tapping the folder on top. "I'm sorry, but I've got a long drive ahead of me."

The heat instantly surrounded the two of them as they walked out of the station house together.

"Why has he decided to start killing *now?*"

Mr. Horner unlocked his car. "That's something I can't answer." He slid behind the wheel and started the engine. "Good luck to you, Chief. If I can help you further, please let me know."

"Well, how about telling the FBI we could use some of their men on this?"

Horner smiled and shook his head. "I will, but don't hold your breath."

Chapter Seven

For the past two years, Nathan had eaten dinner with Jack and Cheryl nearly every Sunday. This was something he found himself always looking forward to as the end of the week drew to a close. They were the closest thing to a family he felt he would ever have.

It also didn't hurt matters that Cheryl happened to be an excellent cook. She hailed from the South where meat and potatoes were a standard.

"This is really good," he said, smiling at her between bites.

A pink hue encompassed her cheeks. "Thank you, Nathan."

"Can you pass the gravy, sweetheart?"

Cheryl turned her attention to Jack as she handed him the bowl. "Did you ask Nathan about helping you?"

He cleared his throat. "Uh, not yet."

Nathan put the last spoonful of potatoes into his mouth and pushed his plate away. "Ask me to help you with what?"

"Nothing," Jack replied, wiping his fingers with a napkin.

Cheryl gave her husband a funny look and then rolled her eyes. "Nathan, do you think you could help him put the crib and the rest of the baby furniture together the next time you come?"

Jack saw him clench and unclench his jaw before forming a small smile.

"Of course," he said, looking at Cheryl. "I'd be glad to help."

After dinner, the two men went outside for a beer.

Nathan sat down on the porch and watched as the sun sank slowly behind the trees. A dog-eared wooden fence lent some much-needed privacy to Jack's backyard, which he noticed, had just been cut. His deputy was meticulous when it came to his lawn. It was no match to his own, which could only be described as unkempt.

One thing that he *was* able to rib him about, however, was the two pallets of bricks that sat off to the right of the tool shed. They had been there since the beginning of spring. "When are you going to get started on your barbeque pit?"

Jack laughed and shook his head. "I don't know. I really thought I'd be done by now," he said, twisting the cap off his bottle. "Maybe after the baby's born, I'll find time to do it."

Nathan flashed him a grin. "Really? You *really* think it's going to work that way?"

"Probably not," he said, shrugging.

Nathan chuckled at his deputy's ignorance before taking a sip of his beer. When he was finished, he saw that the smile had faded from his face. "What's wrong?"

"I was hoping to take some time off when Cheryl has the baby." He sat forward and placed his elbows on his knees. "But that was before all this started."

Nathan sighed. The past five weeks had been horrible, to say the least.

"Do you think we're going to get any outside help on this?"

"Mr. Horner said for us not to hold our breaths." He set his bottle of beer down between his feet. "We've got *four* days, Jack. *Four* days to find this guy before he kills again." He looked over at him and shook his head. "And I don't have a *fucking clue* how to find him."

Jack leaned his shoulder against the porch railing and took another sip from his beer. "Well, tomorrow Hoskins will be back from sick leave. That'll give us an extra man to help canvas the area."

"Yeah," he answered, watching the lightning bugs fill the impending darkness.

"Are you certain this guy's a local?"

"I feel that he is. No out-of-towner would be that familiar with the lake. This guy knows where the high and low points are."

The night waned on as they sat together discussing the six-foot-tall, left-handed killer who got himself off on women's fear.

~

The next morning Nathan and Jack, along with Hoskins, started another sweep of the area where the last victim had been discovered.

There wasn't a blade of grass that hadn't already been looked at, but Nathan held onto the hope that they would find something. As he walked along the bank, he could feel his chest tightening at the thought of finding another victim. He knew he was running out of time.

He stopped near the edge of the trail and cupped his hands around his mouth. "Hey, Hoskins? I want you to go over to the north side and knock on the cabins. See if anybody saw or heard anything that night."

Hoskins wiped his brow with the sleeve of his shirt and nodded. "Okay, Boss."

Nathan watched him trudge back up the slope. His deputy wasn't much on physical labor, but he loved to talk. He could talk to anybody about anything — anytime — anywhere, which made him the perfect choice to speak to the tourists.

Once Hoskins had disappeared from his sight, he turned and looked out over the water. Across the lake was the north side where the cabins were. He could see them from here, stacked together like dominoes.

Just to the right of them was an enormous parking lot that led to the marina. He motioned at Jack who stood a few feet away. "We need to go talk to the owners of the boats. One of them may have heard something."

~

The back of Nathan's shirt stuck to him as he walked along the wooden dock. He had been here for nearly two hours and was, unfortunately, no more ahead than he was this morning.

He'd only managed to speak to about a dozen people so far, as most of the boats had for sale signs posted on them and were empty of occupants.

He stepped over the railing of the next one and knocked on the sliding glass door. There was no answer. Hearing water running up above, he made his way around to the side. "Anybody home?" he shouted.

The water shut off.

Nathan shielded his eyes as he squinted into the sun. After a moment, he saw a man appear.

"Can I help you?"

"I'm Chief Sommers," he said, flashing his badge. "I'd like to ask you some questions."

"Be right down."

A second or two later, the man descended the ladder.

Nathan moved out of the way as he reached the bottom rung.

The man gave him a wary look. "Sean Evans," he said, extending his hand.

"Were you here on your boat last Wednesday?"

He wiped his hands with a rag. "What time Wednesday?"

"Between four in the afternoon and midnight."

The corners of his mouth twitched slightly. "Yeah, I was here, but I wasn't docked. I took the boat out for a cruise that night. Why? Does this have something to do with the murder of that girl?"

Nathan opened his mouth to reply when he saw Jack walking towards him. He was coming at a fast pace. "Excuse me just a moment."

Evans put his hands on his waist and nodded. "Sure."

Nathan stepped back onto the dock, meeting his deputy halfway. "Do you have something?"

Jack glanced sideways at the man before answering. "We've got a witness that swears our victim was on this boat the day she died," he said in a low voice.

Nathan restrained himself from looking back at Evans. He was about to ask Jack if he was sure of this but saw the deliberateness in his eyes.

In a slow and non-threatening manner, Nathan climbed back onto the houseboat with Jack right behind him.

"Mr. Evans," he said, reaching into his shirt pocket for the flyer, "have you ever seen this girl before?" He watched him closely, searching for any subtle movement in his face. Out of the corner of his eye, he saw Jack casually place his hand on his Glock.

Evans was visibly sweating now. "Yeah, I've seen her. She was with me on my boat Wednesday." He handed the flyer back to Nathan. "But I had nothing to do with her death."

"Do you mind if I take a look around?"

He swung his eyes towards Jack. "Do you have a search warrant?"

"No," he answered, shaking his head. "But I can get one within the hour."

Evans gave him a hard look before offering a rigid shrug. "Go ahead. I've got nothing to hide."

Jack exchanged glances with Nathan before disappearing through the sliding door.

"Let's start from the beginning. How did you meet her?"

"I was at the marina Wednesday getting some supplies when I met her inside the store. We talked for a bit and she seemed nice, so I asked her if she wanted to go for a cruise around the lake."

"Then what happened?"

"*Nothing*. We had a nice time, that's all."

"What time did you dock?"

"Around ten-thirty. I was going to walk her back to her cabin, but she said she would be fine."

"You let her go back alone?"

Evans held his hands out to his sides. "I walked her to the marina and opened the gate for her. That was the last time I saw her. I swear."

∼

Two hours later, a very agitated Sean Evans sat in the interrogation room.

"Can anybody verify your whereabouts after you dropped her off?" Nathan stood behind him with his arms crossed.

Evans ran his fingers through his short brown hair. "Not that I know of."

"What did the two of you do the whole time you were together?"

"I've answered that question already," he said through gritted teeth.

The door opened slightly. "Chief?" Jack motioned for him.

Nathan walked around the table and followed him outside.

"The judge signed the search warrant."

"Okay, you and Hoskins go turn that boat upside down."

The initial search by Jack hadn't turned up anything, but if there *was* something to be found, he wanted it to be by the book. He didn't want this guy getting off on a technicality.

He went back inside the room and pulled the chair out across from Evans. "You didn't answer my question."

"Which question was that?"

Nathan put his right leg on the seat and rested his elbow on his knee. "What did the two of you do while you were on the boat?"

"We had some dinner, drank some wine, and talked." His eyes grew dark. "Now that's the *tenth* time I've answered you on that!"

"Did you sleep with her?"

"No."

"Did you try?"

"No."

"Why not?"

"Because she was just coming out of a bad relationship."

Nathan leaned forward as he balanced his foot on the chair. "And?"

Evans clenched his fists. "*And*, I didn't need anybody else's leftovers!"

"So, what does that mean?" he asked, finding his answer strange. "You only like virgins?"

Evans slowly raised his head to meet his gaze. "She told me she was pregnant, okay? I didn't need that complication in my life right now. So, we just talked."

Nathan shoved the chair out of his way and stormed out the door. Once he was in his office, he jerked the phone off its cradle and punched the buttons he knew by heart.

He began pacing the floor as he waited for someone to pick up. "Jean, I need to speak with Doc Jensen." He reached behind him and swung the door shut. "No, it *can't* wait."

"What is it, Nathan?" Harry's disgruntled voice came over the receiver.

"I need you to find out if Missy Rosenberg was pregnant."

There was a slight pause. "All right. I'll ask the lab to include it with the other blood work."

"How long before you know?"

"I can probably have it in a couple of days."

"Thanks, Harry. I owe you one."

"You know, Nathan, I might actually believe you if you sounded like you meant it."

A loud click sounded in Nathan's ear, making him clench his jaw. He pulled Missy Rosenberg's file from the top tray and flipped to the last page. "Norma?" he said, opening his door.

The older woman looked up from her desk.

He held out a piece of paper to her as he drew near. "This is the name of the victim's fiancé. I need for you to get in touch with the police in Wibaux County and ask them to check if he has an alibi for last Wednesday night."

Norma's brown eyes twinkled as she took the slip of paper from him. "I'm on it, Chief."

He gave her a slight smile, knowing that she fancied herself an amateur detective. Turning towards the interrogation room, he could see Evans through the glass window in the door. He was sitting with his head bowed and his hands clasped over the back of his neck.

"What do you do for a living, Mr. Evans?" he asked, walking inside.

He lifted up his head and sighed. "I design websites."

"Do you work here in Silver Creek?"

"They're *websites*," he said, talking to Nathan as if he were stupid. "I can work anywhere I want. All I need is my laptop."

"So you live on your boat?" Nathan asked, closing the door behind him.

"Yeah."

"Year-round?"

"Yeah."

"You probably see a lot of girls down at the marina. A lot of single women."

Evans suddenly stood up. "Look, I get it! I *get* it, okay? I know it looks like I murdered that girl, but I swear to *God*, I had nothing to do with it! I swear to you!"

Unfazed by his outburst, Nathan slid a legal pad in front of him. "I need for you to write down everything that happened from the time you met Missy Rosenberg, until the time you say you dropped her off."

"You don't believe me, do you?"

Nathan tossed a pen on the table. "Don't leave out any detail."

Evans plopped himself back down in the chair and grabbed the pen.

Nathan sighed inwardly as he watched. Evans was right-handed.

He stepped outside, intending to get hold of Missy's friend, Tiffany. Most girls would tell their best friend if they were pregnant, and he wanted to know why she hadn't said anything.

As he headed to his office he glanced over at Norma and saw Mac Hodges perched on the edge of her desk. The hairs on the back of his neck immediately began to bristle. "What are you doing here, Hodges?"

Mac stood up and made his way over. "I came to get an interview from you regarding the latest victim."

"I don't give interviews," he said, slamming the door in his face.

Norma arched her eyebrow as she watched Hodges open the door and walk on in. "The guy's got a death wish," she mumbled under her breath.

"Get out, Hodges."

He held up his hands. "Look, I'm just trying to keep the people of Silver Creek apprised of the situation. Do you have any leads?" His eyes flicked over towards the interrogation room.

Nathan walked around his desk and stood directly in front of him. "Get out."

Hodges shook his head. "The mayor said you would cooperate with me."

He felt his jaw tighten. "Did he?"

"Yeah. Said you would grant me an interview."

"Well, he was mistaken."

Hodges glanced at the interrogation room again. "Who do you have in there?"

Nathan stared down at him. When he spoke, his voice was low. "I'm not going to tell you again."

"All right, *Chief*. I can take a hint. I'll go back and tell Tom that you said he was mistaken."

"You do that."

Hodges left his office and turned towards the interrogation room.

"Chief, do you copy?"

"Stand by, Jack." He pointed his finger towards the exit. "The door's that way."

Hodges smiled at him before ambling towards the door. "See ya around, *Chief*."

Nathan waited until he had actually left the building before speaking into the radio. "Go ahead, Jack."

"We've tossed the boat and can't find anything." There was a long pause. "There's nothing here to link Evans to the girl at all."

Nathan heard the disappointment in his voice. "All right. Come on back. But first, I want you to stop at the marina and see if they remember the victim coming in there on Wednesday."

"10-4."

And just like that, they were back to square one.

Chapter Eight

Nathan took a long sip of coffee as he stared out the window of his office. Earlier this morning, Norma had proudly informed him that Missy's fiancé did have an alibi the night of the murder and that it had been confirmed by the Wibaux authorities.

He clenched his jaw. It had now been eight days since Missy Rosenberg's murder. The killer had struck every eight days for the past month, and he was no closer to catching him than he was before.

On top of that, he felt he had no choice but to release Sean Evans, who had maintained all along that he had nothing to do with her death. The ironic thing was that, indirectly, he did. If Evans *had* slept with her that night, she probably would still be alive today.

Nathan rubbed the back of his neck and sighed. He felt that Missy had been a spontaneous target—a girl who just happened to be at the wrong place at the wrong time.

He took another sip of coffee as he watched the activity outside his window. It was supposed to reach ninety-five today and the boat traffic was already heavy. Several trucks with trailers drove slowly down Main Street and turned right towards the lake.

In the past five minutes, he'd counted at least ten girls pass by. Dressed in short outfits and sandals, they pranced down the sidewalk to the bus stop that would take them to the marina.

Nathan grimaced. He didn't want to see one of them turn up in the morgue. Taking a step closer, he looked around. He knew that some twisted person somewhere was also watching.

Shifting his gaze across the street, he noticed that the cat lady was outside the bakery cleaning the shop's windows, as a man on a ladder worked on hanging a new pink awning in front of the store.

As much as he wanted to, he found that he was unable to stop himself from watching her as she scrubbed the windows. Her arms moved up and down at a furious pace causing certain things to jiggle. His eyes involuntarily moved to her legs. They were lean and tan, highlighted by the white shorts she was wearing. He slowly followed their outline up to her backside—

"Chief?"

He turned so suddenly that he spilled his coffee on his shirt.

Jack saw the redness in his cheeks and glanced out the window.

"What is it, Jack?" he said, trying to wipe the coffee off of him.

"Uh, I've got some information for you."

He set his mug down on his desk. "What?"

"Missy Rosenberg *was* at the marina Wednesday..." Jack looked out the window again trying to determine what had gotten him so flustered.

"*And?*"

"And," he said, returning his attention to him, "the sales clerk remembered that she had reserved two Jet Skis for Thursday afternoon. Here's a copy of the rental receipt."

Nathan studied the paper for a moment. Missy's name and signature were on it.

"The sales clerk at *Sam's* said he remembered her asking about the Jet Skis. But he doesn't remember Evans being there."

Norma poked her head in the doorway. "Sorry to interrupt. But there's a fight at *Carl's Place.*"

~

The brawl was still in progress when Nathan and Jack arrived at the bar. They pushed their way through the crowd of people to find two men throwing punches at one another.

They went to pull them apart, but it was like trying to separate two scrapping dogs.

Nathan took hold of the bigger man and shoved him against the bar. He put his hand against the back of his head, pushing it down until his face touched the counter.

"Let me go," he said, reaching for a bottle of beer that was next to him.

Nathan grabbed his arm, making him drop it. Pinning his elbow behind his back, he twisted it upwards until the man yelped in pain.

The other man involved did not resist as Jack pulled him from the floor. His shirt was bloodied and torn as he swayed unsteadily on his feet.

The man Nathan held still struggled to get loose, leaving him no choice but to handcuff him.

"I didn't do anything wrong!" he spat.

"No? Looks to me like you've done plenty," he said, surveying the bar.

Blood trickled from his nose as his breath fell out of him in angry gasps. He turned his head sideways to look at the man in Jack's custody.

Nathan followed his gaze. It was only then that he recognized the other participant in the fight. Sean Evans stood there with blood dribbling from his mouth and face.

"That *bastard* killed my fiancé!" The man started towards him again.

Evans took a step backward but was too out of breath to speak.

The bar fell silent.

Nathan glanced around the room as he kept the man from advancing. All eyes were now upon Evans. In a town this size, a person could go from presumed innocent to guilty to ostracized in a matter of hours. And it could all be done without ever having to set foot inside a courtroom.

"Let's go," he said, pulling on the man's arm.

They led the two men outside with the crowd following behind them.

Jack climbed into the back seat with Evans, as Nathan put the other man up front with him. Before he could start the engine they were surrounded.

"Is that the killer, Chief?"

"Is he the monster?"

There were too many voices talking over each other for Nathan to distinguish. He turned the steering wheel to the left and pulled away from the curb, making the mob scramble to get out of his way.

~

Nathan stared at the man sitting in front of him in the interrogation room. He was still handcuffed, and still *very* angry.

"What's your name?"

"You know my name," he said in a low voice. "You also know where I live, and where I was the night Missy was murdered!"

Nathan paused. "Why are you here today, Mr. Goldman?"

"I came to get Missy's things from the cabin."

"Didn't her friend Tiffany do that already?"

"She was too upset, she just left everything and rode home with Missy's mother. A buddy of mine dropped me off here, and I was going to drive Tiffany's car home."

"*Carl's* is a long way from the cabins."

Goldman curled his blood-stained lip at him. "I went there because someone told me Evans was inside."

"Who told you?"

He looked away in defiance.

Nathan placed his hands on the table and leaned forward. "Was it your intention to kill Evans?"

"So what if it was?" he said, shrugging. "I'd be doing you a favor."

"Premeditated murder carries a possible life sentence, or death by lethal injection, in the state of Montana."

The muscle in Goldman's jaw twitched. "Are you going to arrest Evans for Missy's murder?"

For a brief moment, Nathan saw the agony in his eyes — then they flickered back to anger.

"Well, are you?"

"He's a person of interest. That's all I can say."

Goldman slumped forward in the chair.

"Missy's mother told us you had broken off the engagement. Why?"

"Things between us just weren't working out," he replied in a clipped tone.

"Can you be a little bit more specific?"

"It's none of your business."

"It is now," Nathan said flatly. "I can keep you here for a very long time, and we can talk. *Or* I can put you in lockup until you're arraigned on assault and battery. Arraignments are on Tuesdays and Thursdays." He checked his watch. "Looks like you just missed it for today."

Goldman shifted in his seat as his face turned crimson. "Missy caught me screwing around a few weeks ago and broke off the engagement."

"Her mother told me that *you* broke up with *her*."

"I guess Missy was embarrassed. She didn't want anyone to know the truth."

The door behind Nathan opened. Norma leaned in and handed him a slip of paper. Her eyes told him to read it right away.

He waited for the door to close before he unfolded the note. After a moment, he glanced up. "Did you know that Missy was pregnant?"

Goldman looked confused. "She was pregnant?" He swallowed hard and began shaking his head.

Nathan tucked the note in his shirt pocket. "Who told you where to find Evans?"

He didn't answer. He seemed to be trying to process what he had just told him.

"Who told you where Evans was?" he asked once more.

A sigh fell from his lips as his eyes began to water. "Some reporter. I don't remember his name."

~

Jack was finishing up administering some first aid to Evans in the men's restroom when Nathan walked in. Evans was sitting in a chair with the back of his head resting against the tile wall. His left eye was nearly swollen shut, and he had two Steri-strips covering his left cheek.

"He's no worse for the wear," Jack said, closing the kit.

Nathan folded his arms against his chest. "Do you want to press charges against Goldman?"

Evans stood up. "Yeah! I'd love to press charges against that *asshole!* But what good would that do *me?*" He leaned over and spat a chunk of blood mixed with saliva into the sink. "Can I go now?"

Jack escorted him to the door and opened it for him. "I'd stay out of public places for a while if I were you."

Evans stopped and shot him a look before storming out.

Jack turned towards Nathan and shook his head. "I kind of feel sorry for the guy."

Nathan sat on the edge of the sink. "Goldman told me some reporter approached him and told him where he could find Evans."

"Hodges," Jack said with a sigh. "I bet he was in the bar the entire time."

He nodded. "This type of thing is right up his alley."

Jack held the door open for him. "Do you want me to cut Goldman loose?"

"Not yet," he said walking out. "I'm waiting on the estimate for the damages done to the bar. The owner said he'd have it within the hour." He checked his watch. "Why don't we grab a bite to eat?"

"Chief?" Norma pushed the hold button on the phone. "The mayor wants to speak with you."

"I'll call him back," he said, heading towards the exit.

~

Lunch was anything but pleasant. The two of them had been approached by at least a half-dozen people in the diner who had asked if Evans was the killer.

The sun beat down relentlessly as they crossed the street and began walking the two blocks back to the station house.

Jack glanced around, making sure they were out of earshot before speaking. "Did Jensen confirm that Missy Rosenberg was pregnant?"

"According to the blood test, she was about five weeks along."

Jack sidestepped a power walker. "She must have just found out herself, then."

They continued on in silence for a bit.

"So, where do we go from here?"

Nathan shook his head slightly. "Go back over the files, canvas the areas again, and hope to God we find something." He knew that's not what his deputy wanted to hear, but he honestly didn't have any other answers.

Jack pursed his lips. "I'll take Hoskins out with me this afternoon. We'll start at the cabins again and work our way towards the marina." As he spoke, he noticed Nathan's pace had slowed and that he was staring across the street.

"That sounds like a good start," he replied, turning his attention back to him.

Jack suddenly stopped and gave him a curious look.

"*What?*"

"Why don't you just go over there and introduce yourself?"

Nathan felt his face turning red.

"Go on." Jack nudged him with his elbow.

"Would you *stop*? I can't go over there."

"Why not?"

He sighed. "Well, for one thing, she hates me. That's the cat lady."

"Mmm," Jack said, frowning. "Well, maybe she's over it."

"*No*, I don't think she is."

He placed his hand on his shoulder. "Look, just go on over and talk to her. What's the worst that could happen?"

Nathan shook his head, not wanting to find out.

"Just walk over and welcome her to town. You know, do your chief of police bit." To Jack's surprise, Nathan actually looked as if he were considering it. "Go ahead," he said, giving him a shove in the right direction.

With his heart in his mouth, Nathan started across the street. His legs felt like they were going to buckle beneath him as he stepped onto the sidewalk. He rested his hand on the door to the bakery and looked over his shoulder.

Jack stood on the other side giving him a thumbs up.

Katie was in the process of wiping down a table when she heard the bell above the door ring. "Chief Sommers."

"Hi—" He cleared his throat. "Hi...it's Ms. Winstead, right?"

"Katie," she answered, drying her hands on the towel that was slung over her shoulder. She watched as he began moving towards her in what could only be described as an awkward gait. "What can I do for you?"

"Um, I just wanted to welcome you to Silver Creek. I didn't realize you had bought the bakery."

"Yeah," she said, offering him a small smile. "I've been shopping around for an established bakery for a couple of years now. One that already had the equipment and was in a good location. This place fit the bill perfectly."

"It's nice," he said, looking around.

Katie watched his eyes flit nervously about the room for close to thirty seconds or so. "What can I do for you?" she repeated, wanting to get back to her cleaning.

His eyes immediately stopped roaming and fell upon her. They were intense and blue and caused a warmth to spread across her cheeks.

"I'm sorry about the other day," he mumbled. "I know we didn't get off on the right foot."

She tucked a strand of hair behind her ear and shook her head. "I'm the one who should be apologizing. I didn't mean to behave so rudely towards you. I was just really upset."

"I understand."

The conversation quickly faltered, causing an uncomfortable silence to swarm them.

"You know," she said, saying the first thing that popped into her mind, "you don't look like a cop."

"No?"

"No. Small town cops usually have big bellies and wear cowboy hats."

He grinned at her, revealing an adorable dimple in the middle of his chin.

She couldn't help but smile back.

"Where are you from?" he asked.

"Originally, I'm from Seattle, but the past few years, I've lived in Billings."

"The big city, huh?"

She laughed. "That's right."

The bell rang again.

Looking past the chief's shoulder, she could see a man with a velvety black beard coming towards them. "Can I help—"

"What do you want, Hodges?"

Katie's gaze went from the stranger to Chief Sommers, whose body had grown rigid.

"Good afternoon, ma'am," he said, making it a point to step around the chief. "I just wanted to know if you were open. I've got a hankering for something sweet."

"I'm sorry, I'm not operating yet. But please come back on Friday. That's my grand opening."

He gave her a broad smile. "I'll be sure to." As he turned to go, he glanced sideways at Chief Sommers. "*Chief.*"

Katie could almost see him bristle as the man walked past him and out the door. "Is everything all right?"

"Everything's fine," he said, shifting his attention back to her.

She tilted her head, not really sure that she believed him.

He unclenched his jaw—and his fists. "I better get back to work."

Before she could tell him goodbye, he turned and began walking away.

~

When Nathan returned to the station, Jack was waiting for him like a giddy schoolgirl. "How'd it go?"

"Good," he said, forcing a smile. Looking past him, he noticed the door to the interrogation room was open. "Did you let Goldman go?"

"Yeah. We got the estimate from *Carl's*. He paid for it in cash and stormed out about five minutes ago."

Hoskins came up and slapped Jack across the shoulders. "Ready to go, Collins?"

Jack gave Nathan a nod as he pushed open the door. "We'll let you know if we find anything."

"Chief?"

He turned around.

"The mayor's office has called three times."

He took the pink slips of paper from Norma and stalked back to his office, slamming the door behind him. Seeing Mac in the bakery just now had reignited feelings inside of him that he had tried his best to forget. He let his hand rest on his waist as a bitter sigh fell from his lips. Even if he could let it go…he knew that Mac never would.

His door suddenly opened.

"Why haven't you returned my calls?"

"I've been a little busy," he said, not bothering to look over.

"What part of *daily report* didn't you understand?" asked Manning, pushing the door closed.

Nathan stared at the map on his wall, refusing to answer.

"I heard that you arrested a suspect on Monday."

"I didn't make any *arrests*. He's a person of interest, that's all," he said, wondering how the hell he'd found out about Evans in the first place.

"Why didn't you charge him?"

"No evidence was found linking him to any of the murders. If I charged him, the case would've been thrown out before it ever went to trial." He shook his head. "Besides, he's not our killer."

"You sure about that?"

"I'm positive."

"You know something, Sommers?" Manning said, taking a step closer to him. "Three years ago I would've taken you on your word alone. But now…"

"Now, you have your doubts," Nathan finished for him.

"You were a top detective. One of the best. You came with a packet full of accommodations. But ever since these murders started," he said, gesturing with his hand, "you act like you don't even care."

Nathan cocked his head. "I don't *care?* I've been working my *ass* off on this case!"

"No, you've been doing this *half-ass!* From what I've heard Evans looked good for it!"

"Where did you get your detective's license?" he asked in a low voice.

Manning glanced away for a moment. "Look, Nathan…I'm not trying to tell you how to do your job—"

"Then *don't*," he said. "And don't go granting interviews with Hodges on my behalf."

"I've got to answer to the public. They want to know what's going on. What am I supposed to tell them?"

"You're a politician. Make something up."

Manning's jaw twitched. "That's not fair, Nathan."

He turned away and bowed his head. "I've got a killer to catch, Tom. I'd appreciate it if you'd let me get to it."

A swift breeze surrounded him as the door opened and slammed.

Nathan closed his eyes, trying to shut everything out but the problem at hand. He stood in the middle of his office, unmoving, for a long time. There was no way he could face coming in here tomorrow, knowing that a girl was probably going to die tonight.

Chapter Nine

Nathan held his fishing rod between his knees as he slipped a chicken liver onto its hook. He didn't like the smell, or *feel* of it, but it was better than impaling a worm and watching it writhe in agony while it slowly drowned.

With a quick flick of his wrist, he cast his line out about fifteen feet from the shore. The liver made a small plopping sound as it hit the water. He set the bottom of his rod in the holder and leaned back against the trunk of a willow tree.

He could feel the air, heavy with dew, settling on the grass beside him as he watched the night descend around Graves Landing.

His anger was still fresh over the conversation he'd had earlier with the mayor. Perhaps the reason he was so angry was because deep down, he knew Manning was right. The past couple of years he had become apathetic towards a lot of things in his life — his job being one of them.

Across the lake, near the north shore, the beginnings of laughter and music could be heard as the nightlife at the cabins started up.

The moon was so low it looked as if it had dipped into the lake; its reflection spilled silently across the water casting a silver glow.

Nathan breathed in deeply as he listened to the frogs and crickets talking amongst themselves. There was a certain innocence to fishing. Maybe it was because it reminded him of happier times.

When he was a boy, he used to spend the summers with his father in Carlsbad. Sometimes he would wake him before dawn and they would head down to the pier and charter a boat. Nathan could still see himself standing on its deck, watching the shoreline grow smaller and smaller as they headed out to sea.

He rubbed his eyes for a moment. Maybe it wasn't the fishing he enjoyed as much as getting to spend time with his father. Nathan had always been able to talk to him about anything. He was a very kind and understanding man; slow to temper, and quick to forgive.

A sigh fell from his lips. He had died nearly ten years ago, and there wasn't a day that went by that he didn't miss talking with him.

~

The hours slowly passed as he sat underneath the tree, waiting and listening. The cabins had all grown quiet, indicating to him that the singles had mingled, and were now either sleeping with their chosen one or passed out drunk. Graves Landing had become eerily silent—even the crickets had stopped chirping.

The quiet, coupled with the mugginess, caused his eyelids to grow heavy. His thoughts inevitably turned to Jenny as sleep surrounded him.

Nathan could still see her sitting at their kitchen table. Her head was bowed, and her fingers were spread over her mouth.

He stood solemnly in front of her, his own hands trembling as he looked at the photos she had given him just moments earlier.

"I asked you a question, Nathan."

"No," he whispered.

She slowly lifted her head, her eyes searching his face.

"I didn't sleep with her."

She got to her feet and drew a quivering breath as tears began spilling down her cheeks.

"I didn't."

She came around the table and jerked the photos out of his hand. "Pictures don't lie, Nathan!"

"Who are you going to believe, Jenny?" He reached out and grasped her by the shoulders. "Me? Or that ex-boyfriend of yours?"

She pushed against his chest making him let go. "Don't you dare twist this around!" she yelled, flinging the photos back at him.

He clenched his jaw and put his hands on his waist.

"Do you love her?"

"No. I don't love her," he said, looking up. "And I didn't sleep with her."

Her eyes flooded. "I know when you're lying, Nathan." She suddenly buried her face in her hands as her shoulders began to shake.

Nathan picked one of the photos up from off the floor and crumpled it in his fingers.

"I never thought you would do this to me," she sobbed.

He reached out for her. "Jenny…"

She pushed his hands aside and snatched her keys from off the counter.

"Where are you going?"

She ran out the front door towards her car.

He caught up to her and grabbed her by the arm. "Where are you going?"

"I don't know. I just need to get away from you right now." She slid into the seat and started the engine.

"Jenny, please."

She shifted the car into reverse and backed down the driveway.

"Jenny!" His hands fell helplessly to his sides as he watched her race down the street before rounding the corner.

Time either sped up or slowed down, as he stood in their driveway. He couldn't tell which. He heard his cell phone ringing, but couldn't bring himself to answer it.

"Nathan?"

He was suddenly standing in the middle of Blossom Lane. Red and blue lights were flashing all around him as the smell of smoke filled his throat.

"Nathan?"

He rubbed his eyes, trying to clear the fog from them. When he opened them, Jack was standing in front of him, his face more troubled than he'd ever seen it.

Looking past him, he saw the mangled wreckage that lay up against a huge tree. Smoke billowed out from underneath the crumpled hood. The driver's side window was smashed, and he could see her slumped over the steering wheel, unmoving.

He stumbled around Jack and ran towards the car.

Jack scrambled to get in front of him. "Nathan, I can't let you see her," he said, grabbing him by his shirt and holding him tight. "It's better this way."

Nathan shook his head. "No…"

Jack's eyes began to fill with tears. "It's better this way," he whispered.

A sob broke loose from Nathan's throat as he sank to his knees, pulling Jack with him. "No!"

"I'm sorry, Nathan. I'm so sorry."

He clutched at Jack's arms as he wept. "No…no…Jenny!"

He woke himself up screaming her name. It took him a moment to realize where he was as he looked out into the darkness. He wiped his eyes with the sleeve of his t-shirt and waited for the dream to leave him.

The sound of a trolling motor just off the shore made him jerk his head up. A few yards ahead he could just make out the shape of a small johnboat. It was moving at a very slow pace.

He could see a light coming from it as it drew closer to the bank. As it passed underneath the silhouette of the moon, he could discern a dark figure.

Nathan quietly got to his feet and reached for his flashlight, but before he could turn it on, the light from the boat suddenly shined in his eyes. He instinctively dropped down and pulled his gun.

"Chief? Is that you?"

Nathan hesitated and then shined his own light into the boat. After a moment, he holstered his gun. "What are you doing out here, Sam?"

He squinted against the beam. "Lookin' for frogs. I've gotten some big ones tonight." He reached beside him in the boat and held up a bullfrog by its leg.

Nathan followed Bryant's hand with the light until it came to rest on the frog. Its lifeless body dangled from his fingers.

"What about you? You havin' any luck?"

Nathan didn't answer at first, not sure as to what he was asking.

"What kind of bait are you using?"

"Chicken livers."

"Next time, try night crawlers."

Nathan nodded, but then realized Bryant couldn't see him. "I will," he answered.

"Have a good night, Chief."

"You too." The ripples lapped silently at the shore as he watched Sam guide his boat farther down the bank.

Chapter Ten

The sun had risen by the time Nathan arrived home. He stopped in his kitchen to fill the coffee maker and then made his way down the hall towards the bathroom.

Hot water sprayed on the back of his neck as he leaned against the shower stall and closed his eyes. He didn't know if his presence at the lake last night had done any good or not. He still halfway expected a phone call this morning, and found himself cringing at the thought.

He stepped out of the shower and wrapped a towel around his waist. As he lathered his face with shaving cream, he mentally began going over his day. It was Friday, which always meant increased traffic coming to town for the weekend. That meant more headaches for him and his deputies.

He drew the razor across his chin. There was also a stack of reports to go over and sign, along with budget requests and requisitions to fill out. He thought of about a dozen other things he had to take care of as he rinsed his face.

He suddenly caught sight of his reflection. A man he barely recognized stared back. Jenny had once told him that his eyes were a vibrant blue. He placed his hands on the sink and leaned in close. They looked dull and gray to him.

The coffee pot let out a small sigh indicating it was done. Nathan sighed along with it as he turned to get dressed. Standing here wasn't going to accomplish anything.

~

Jack sat on the edge of Norma's desk sipping his coffee. Hoskins was stretched out in the chair in front of her with his feet propped up. It was a morning routine for them. Good coffee and quiet conversation before the chaos ensued.

Norma stirred a small amount of cream into her mug. "So, Jack, how many more weeks?"

"Six."

"Better enjoy the peace and quiet while you can, Collins," Hoskins said, nudging him with his foot, "because life as you know it will soon cease to exist."

He grinned at him. "That's what everybody keeps telling me."

The bell to the front door jingled.

A woman came in carrying a large pink box in her arms. A smaller one, tied up with string, hung from her fingertips.

Jack stood up and walked over to her. "Good morning."

She clutched the box in her hands and smiled nervously. "My name's Katie Winstead. I'm the new owner of the bakery across the street."

"Nice to meet you. I'm Jack, this is Norma, and that guy over there is Si."

She nodded at them. "I've brought you some donuts this morning. Today is my grand opening."

Hoskins came around the desk and took the box from her. "Smells divine," he said, taking a deep breath.

They all watched as he shoved nearly two-thirds of a Long john into his mouth.

He chewed for a moment and then fluttered his eyes. "I've died and gone to heaven."

"You're *gonna* die all right if you keep shoveling those in," scolded Norma.

"I'll have you know I got a clean bill of health last week," he said, taking another bite.

The bell chimed again and the four of them turned to look.

Nathan stopped in his tracks upon seeing Katie.

"Good morning, Chief Sommers," she said, giving him a warm smile.

"Morning."

She held the small box out to him. "I brought you something."

He glanced at his deputies before taking it. "Thanks." Quietness suddenly enveloped the station as he fumbled for something to say.

"Would you like some coffee, Katie?" Jack intervened.

"Oh, no thank you. I better get back over to the shop. It was nice meeting all of you."

"Thanks for the donuts, Katie," Hoskins said, giving her a wave.

Jack watched him pop another one into his mouth. "You know those are for all of us, right?"

Nathan lunged for the door. "Here. Let me get that for you."

"Thank you, Chief."

"Call me Nathan," he said, walking outside with her.

"All right. Thank you, Nathan."

As he stood on the landing with her, he became keenly aware of the three pairs of eyes that were staring at him through the front window. "Thank you for the donuts," he said, taking a step to his right to block her from seeing them.

"I think he likes her," Norma mused as the three of them watched from the inside.

After a few minutes, Katie nodded goodbye to him and hurried across the street.

When Nathan walked back into the station, they turned from the window to look at him.

"What?"

"Nothing," they answered in unison.

Nathan's face matched the box Katie had given him as he took it into his office and closed the door.

Hoskins arched his eyebrow. "Oh, yeah. He's got it bad for her."

~

Later that morning, Nathan was at the docks investigating a burglary. He'd had every intention of hiding in his office and catching up on paperwork, but Jack had a full day in court, and Hoskins was on traffic detail.

"Is there anything else missing besides the generator?" he asked, walking around the deck of the boat.

"No, that's all they took," the elderly man said, scratching his head.

"Are you insured, Dr. Adams?"

"I've got insurance for the boat, but I don't know if the generator's covered or not. I'll have to call my agent."

Nathan made his way over to the railing. "Well, your best bet is to file a claim and have the agency reimburse you. I've got your serial number," he said, tapping his pen against the clipboard, "but honestly, it's probably out of the county by now."

"Yeah, that's what I figured."

"I'm sorry for your trouble. You can stop by tomorrow and pick up a copy of the police report."

"You know, I've owned this boat for eight years now, and this is the first time anything's ever been stolen."

"Is that right?"

"Why do you suppose that is?"

Nathan sighed. Dr. Adams was a retired dentist who loved to talk. If he didn't break off the conversation now, he could easily be here for another hour. He really wished Hoskins were here.

"Is this just the type of society we live in today?"

He swung his leg over the rail. "Can't really say. Be sure to check on your insurance now." Nathan quickly walked away from the boat, not waiting for a reply.

By the time he neared the end of the dock, his pace had slowed to normal. As he passed by Sean Evans' boat, he couldn't help noticing the for sale sign taped to its window.

He climbed onto the deck and could see Evans inside packing up.

Evans looked over his shoulder. His eye was still swollen and had turned a deep purple. "What do you want, Chief Sommers?" His disposition was the same as the last time they'd spoken.

Nathan stepped inside the cabin. "I see you're selling the boat."

He turned his attention back to what he was doing. "Yeah, well, I can't see any reason to stay." He stopped packing and glanced up. "I heard old man Adams lost his generator. You here to interrogate me about that, too?"

"No, but I do have one final question about Missy Rosenberg," he said evenly.

Evans folded his arms across his chest. "What's that?"

"Why do you think Missy confided in you that she was pregnant? Her fiancé and best friend didn't even know. Why would she tell a total stranger?"

He shook his head and shrugged. "I don't know. If I knew the way women worked, I'd be a rich man."

"Well, I'll let you get back to your packing." Nathan started to go but stopped. "I also wanted to tell you that I'm sorry for what happened. I hope you can understand that it was nothing personal. I was just doing my job."

Evans put his hands on his hips. "Well, I hope *you* understand for my not accepting your apology."

Chapter Eleven

Sunday afternoon, Nathan sat hunched over his desk at the station diligently catching up on his paperwork. The phone had not rung at all today, which had allowed him to get more than halfway through the stack of reports.

Upon finishing the budget request, he signed his name and leaned back in his chair. Asking for the money for another deputy was completely justified, but he knew that Manning would probably deny it.

There were times that he missed the simplicity of being a detective in Sacramento. He did his job and answered only to his captain, who took all the crap and dealt with the politics.

He straightened up and stretched for a moment. Fortunately, there had been no murder this past week, but thinking there might be, had left him visibly on edge, causing everyone around him to give him a wide berth.

He stared solemnly at the folders in the tray. He didn't know if the killer had moved on, or was just waiting. Once more, he pulled them out and laid them in front of him. He pored over each victim's file, comparing them to the other three, hoping to find a connection.

The first victim's photo haunted him more than the others. Carol Fuqua was the only one who had been a local. She honestly just didn't seem to fit. The second victim had been a twenty-five-year-old African American woman. Like the third and fourth victims, she was vacationing in one of the cabins with her girlfriend.

He sighed and closed the files. Tomorrow, he would send Hoskins over to talk to the owner of the cabins. As he placed the folders back in the tray, he caught sight of the time on his watch. Jack and Cheryl were expecting him fifteen minutes ago.

~

"Come on in, Nathan," Cheryl said, greeting him with a kiss to the side of his face.

"Sorry I'm late."

Jack came into the foyer wearing a nervous smile.

He noticed the odd expression his deputy wore and was about to ask him what was wrong when Cheryl motioned behind him.

"Katie?"

Nathan turned sharply, bumping his elbow against her breast. "I'm sorry," he said, feeling a familiar warmth circle his cheeks.

"That's okay," Katie replied, taking a small step backward.

"As I understand it, the two of you already know each other?"

"That's right," she said, nodding at Cheryl.

"It's nice to see you again, Katie," Nathan said after a moment.

The silence grew, entangling the four of them.

Cheryl wiped her hands on the towel she was carrying. "Dinner's almost ready," she said, heading back into the kitchen. "Katie, would you mind helping me?"

"Of course not."

Jack turned to follow them, but Nathan grabbed his arm.

"I swear I didn't do this," he said in a hushed whisper. "Cheryl did it all on her own."

Nathan narrowed his eyes at him. "How did she know about her, then?"

He shrugged innocently. "I don't know."

"You're one of the worst liars I've ever known, Jack!"

"Okay, *fine*! I may have said something to Cheryl about her, but that was it! She went down to the bakery and invited her. *Not* me!"

"Why did she do that?"

"Would you keep your voice down?" he said, glancing towards the kitchen.

"Why would she do that?" Nathan repeated in an angry whisper.

"I don't know! *She's seven-and-a-half-months pregnant!* She doesn't think *rationally* anymore!"

"Time to eat!" called Cheryl.

Nathan clenched his jaw as he made his way into the kitchen.

"Here you are, Nathan," Cheryl said, patting the chair that happened to be directly across from Katie.

He begrudgingly took a seat.

"It smells good, sweetheart," Jack said, trying to force the tension out of the room.

"Thank you," she said, handing the plate of rolls to him.

Katie unfolded her napkin and placed it in her lap. "How long have you and Jack been married?" she asked, keeping her eyes focused on Cheryl.

"Almost two years now."

Nathan filled his plate, hoping he wasn't going to be asked to participate in this question and answer session.

"How did the two of you meet?"

A broad grin broke out over Jack's face as he took a bite of meatloaf.

Cheryl shook her head. "He pulled me over for speeding."

"You're kidding?"

"No. That's the honest truth," she said in her southern drawl.

Jack wiped his mouth. "I was driving down Birchwood one afternoon when this woman in a red Mustang goes flying by."

Nathan silently listened to the two of them telling their story. He had heard it several times over, but never grew tired of it. He found it amusing the way they each took turns telling certain parts.

He shifted his gaze to Katie as she sat listening. After a moment, she threw her head back and laughed.

"Then he calls me the next day and asks me out on a date."

"Weren't you mad at him for giving you the ticket?"

"*Oh, yes,*" Jack said, cocking his left eyebrow.

Cheryl reached over and patted his face. "Yes, I was. But he was just too darn cute to say no to."

Katie smiled at them. "That's so sweet!"

"Just think," Jack said, winking at his wife. "If I hadn't pulled you over that day, we might never have met."

"I know," she said nodding. "Fate's funny isn't it?" She turned her attention to her guest. "So, Katie, tell me how you and Nathan met." She was hoping to draw Nathan in on the conversation, who up until now had remained silent.

Jack cleared his throat and shot her a look.

Cheryl shrugged. "*What?* It's a simple question."

"Well," Katie said. "It's not as cute of a story as yours."

Nathan twisted uncomfortably in his chair.

"The day after I moved into my house, my cat was killed by my neighbor's stupid dog. Nathan handled the call."

"Oh, I'm so sorry." Cheryl began shaking her head.

Nathan stared at the table as Katie recounted the story of how her cat was murdered. That was her terminology, not his. He heard her voice start to quiver, and looked up to see that her eyes were brimming with tears. He then shifted his gaze over to Cheryl, who was staring at him like it was all *his* fault that her cat was dead.

When the harrowing account was over, a long silence ensued.

"Katie, did I see you bring in a cheesecake?" Jack asked, wanting to put the subject behind them.

She smiled and wiped at her eyes. "It's strawberry."

He leaned back in his chair. "I can't wait to taste it."

Throughout the rest of dinner, the conversation ebbed and flowed. Afterwards, they migrated to the living room for coffee and dessert.

Cheryl and Katie talked about various things before the subject eventually turned to babies and impending motherhood.

Jack sat on the sofa next to his wife, listening to the two of them. Every now and then, he would place his hand on her stomach and rub it.

Nathan watched silently, remembering the first time he'd ever felt the baby move inside Jenny.

They were gathered at her father's house for a huge dinner party, and for the past half-hour, he had been seated at this long banquet table making idle conversation with people he barely knew.

He discreetly went to check his watch but saw Jenny glaring at him. He looked at her apologetically and sighed as Manning began telling his Marlin story again. This was at least a fifteen-minute tale – twenty if he dragged it out.

Nathan honestly didn't understand how she could be related to this man. All he could figure was that she must have been switched at birth.

Jenny suddenly took his hand and placed it on her stomach. He glanced over, silently questioning her with his eyes.

She just smiled and moved his hand a little lower.

Then he felt it. A grin broke out over his face as his heart began to melt.

It was one of the most intimate moments he had ever shared with her, even though the room was filled with people. A sense of loss, stronger than he'd ever felt before, came over him.

"Nathan?"

He suddenly stood up, trying to shove it away.

"Are you all right?"

He managed to look over at Cheryl and nod. "I need to be getting on home."

She scooted to the edge of the cushion, and with a little help from Jack, got to her feet. "Would you mind giving Katie a ride?"

He resisted the urge to glare at her, putting on his false smile, instead. "Of course not."

~

Katie sat as far away from Nathan as she possibly could as they drove down the street. "I'm sorry about all of this," she murmured, keeping her eyes straight ahead.

"It's no problem, really," he replied, slowing down as he neared her house.

"I mean, I'm sorry about dinner. I could tell by the look on your face that you weren't expecting me to be there."

Clearly caught off guard by her observation, he fumbled through his mind for something to say.

"You don't talk much, do you?"

He pulled into her driveway and shut off the engine. "It's been a while since I've done this."

"Well," she said, pulling on the handle, "thanks for the ride."

Nathan opened his own door and scrambled around to help her out.

"Thank you."

He escorted her up the steps and instinctively glanced behind him in the darkness as she reached into her purse for her keys.

"Well, thanks again," she said, unlocking the door.

"Katie?"

"Yes?" she asked, looking over her shoulder.

He drew a deep breath. "I really *am* sorry about your cat."

She stared at him blankly as she held onto the knob.

Finding her response less than encouraging, he muttered goodnight and hurried down the steps.

~

Cheryl lay back against the pillow and pulled the covers up around her, trying her best to get comfortable. She flopped over onto her side, longing for the day she could sleep on her stomach again.

Jack came out of the bathroom and sat down on the edge of the bed.

"Are you mad at me?" she asked, watching him set the alarm on the clock.

He looked at her over his shoulder and sighed. "No."

"Do you think Nathan is?"

"Uh, yeah. That's a given," he said, slipping under the covers.

She began to feel miserable. "This is the first girl he's shown any interest in. I was just trying to help."

Jack lifted his arm, allowing her to snuggle against him. "I know," he said, kissing her softly on the top of her head. "You were just playing matchmaker."

"Do you think he'll ever forgive me?"

"I'm sure he will in time."

"Well, *that's* comforting."

"When I get home from work tomorrow, I'll see if I can get the crib put together," he said, wanting to change the subject. Her hormones were all over the place, and he knew that if he didn't get her mind off of it, she was going to be weeping in a matter of seconds.

"Okay, but you're on your own tomorrow night for dinner. I have to work."

"Cheryl," he said with a sigh, "we've talked about this. I don't want you working there at night. Not when this guy is still out there."

"It's just one night, Jack. The night manager is on vacation this week. I told you that. Remember?"

"Yes, I remember. And I also remember telling you that I didn't want you doing it."

She raised herself up on her elbow and smiled. "You don't have anything to worry about. I don't think I'm his type."

His expression grew serious. "*The Dollar Mart* is close to the lake. I just want you to be careful. I don't want anything to happen to you."

She laid her head on his chest. "Nothing's going to happen to me, Jack," she said, knowing that these murders were weighing heavily upon him. "I'll be careful. I promise."

~

Nathan sat on his back porch gazing into the darkness. He was still upset with Cheryl for setting him up like that, but in the back of his mind, he knew that she had only done it because she cared.

She and Jack were kind, decent people, who would give you everything they owned if they felt it would make a difference in your life. And they *had* made a difference to him. He knew he wouldn't have gotten through Jenny's death if it hadn't been for the two of them — especially those first few weeks.

He leaned his head against the porch column and closed his eyes as the memories came flooding to the top.

Nathan stared off into the distance as his deputy sat quietly beside him on the steps.

"Were you able to get your mower fixed?" asked Jack in a soft voice.

He shifted his gaze to his backyard, which was ankle-deep. "Not yet."

"You know...it's been three weeks. Do you think that...you might come back to work soon?"

Nathan looked away and shook his head. "I don't know if I'm going to come back."

Jack took a sip of his beer and began picking at the label. "Nathan, I fully understand why you would want to leave Silver Creek. But right now, you're not thinking clearly."

"I'm thinking clearly enough," he said glancing over at him. "In fact, that's all I've been doing, is thinking. I don't belong here anymore."

"I know you feel like going away is the best thing, but you won't be leaving this behind. Grief follows you wherever you go. The only thing that eases the pain is time."

"And distance," Nathan added, pressing the bottle to his lips.

"You're a hell of a police chief, you know."

"I was a better detective."

Jack rested his elbows on his knees and sighed. "So, your mind's made up then?"

He nodded.

"Will you at least stick around long enough to be my best man?"

"You know I will," he said, giving him a small smile.

Neither one of them spoke for a while.

Eventually, Jack patted him on his back and stood up. "I'll see you later."

Nathan cleared his throat. "Thanks for the beer."

Jack stepped off the porch and disappeared around the side of the house.

A moment later, Nathan heard his truck start up. He emptied his beer onto the grass and went inside.

~

The evening turned to dusk and eventually drifted to morning, which then dragged into the afternoon. Having no reason, or desire, to get up, Nathan still lay in bed with his head under the covers.

He knew if he was going to leave Silver Creek, he had to start making some plans — and money. Due to the fact that he'd exhausted all of his bereavement and sick days, his salary from the police department had stopped, causing his savings account to dwindle.

He thought about calling his old captain in Sacramento and asking if he could get back into Homicide. It would be the easiest thing to do.

He brought his head out from under the covers and turned over on his back. There would be a lot of questions, though. His fellow detectives all knew Jenny and knew that they'd gotten married. The thought of having to tell anyone that she had died made him sick.

A sigh fell from his lips. He should go where no one knew him at all. He needed a clean slate.

Knock-Knock!

Nathan remained still, hoping that whoever was at his front door would go away. After a moment, he heard the screen door open and close. He swung his legs over the side of the bed and peered through the blinds. The mailman was walking away.

Slipping on his jeans, he made his way into the living room and opened the door. A small package fell against his feet. He picked it up and turned it over. It was addressed to Jenny.

He leaned against the wall as he tore at the seal. Reaching inside, he pulled out a small article of clothing. It was a pink sleeper with a little yellow duck printed on it. Nathan shoved it back inside the package, not wanting to see it. He carried it through the living room and down the hall to the closed door on the right.

He silently turned the knob and looked in. It still took his breath each time he saw the nursery. Jenny had painted it a light pink during a weekend when she'd had a burst of energy. She was probably one of the most organized people he'd ever known and had already gotten just about everything they needed.

He laid the package down on the dresser next to a pink elephant. His eyes began to sting as he caressed the tip of its trunk with his fingers.

"Just think, Nathan. In less than two months, we're going to be parents!"

He turned and looked behind him. There was no one there, yet he could hear Jenny's words as if she had just spoken them.

"Are you happy, Nathan?"

"Of course I am," he said softly.

She reached up and touched the side of his face. "Well, I know you really wanted a son."

"It doesn't matter to me," he said, drawing her close.

She wrapped her arms around his neck and looked at him for a long time. "Is everything all right?"

"What do you mean?"

"You just...for the past few weeks, you just haven't been yourself."

His smile faded. "I'm fine."

"Are you nervous about being a father?"

He bent down and nuzzled her neck, burying his face in her long blonde locks so she couldn't see him. "Not at all. I can't wait." Guilt overwhelmed him as he hugged her tightly. "I love you so much."

Nathan opened his eyes and swallowed the lump that had formed in his throat. He poured what was left of his beer into the grass and went back inside the house. His steps were slow and unsteady as he made his way down the hallway.

With a trembling hand, he pushed open the door to the nursery and flipped on the light. The package still lay beside the elephant where he had placed it nearly two years ago.

He walked slowly up to the crib and peered over the rail. It was empty and devoid of life...just like he was. He turned and looked behind him, hoping to see her, but the only thing he found was guilt. It was as familiar as it was harsh and began coursing through his veins like fire.

Nathan gripped the edge of the rail as it settled into his heart. Dark and unforgiving, it spread into every crevice of his soul — and just like his grief — he knew that it was never going to leave him.

Chapter Twelve

The following afternoon, Katie stood over her counter preparing to make a batch of double chocolate chip cookies. The recipe was her grandmother's, but over the years, she had tweaked it enough to call it her own.

Her grandmother had always told her that if a person was going to spend over one-third of their life working to earn a living, they best do something they enjoyed. For Katie, this was *it*.

She poured a generous helping of chocolate chips into the batter and began to stir, wishing that her grandmother could be here to see it. She liked to think that she would have been proud of her.

As she folded a cup of sugar into the batter, she counted the number of times the bell over the front door rang. One just now — six in the last hour. Business wasn't booming but had been steady since her grand opening.

"Katie?"

"Yeah?"

A slender girl with brown eyes and matching hair appeared in the doorway. "There's someone here to see you."

"Thanks. I'll be right out."

The girl nodded and disappeared.

Mary had just started working for her this week. She was a nice girl. Maybe a little on the quiet side, but a good worker nonetheless. Most importantly, however, was the fact that she didn't seem to mind the low wages.

Nathan cleared his throat trying to erase the dryness in it as he stood in front of the counter. When it didn't help, he did it again but quickly stopped, feeling like he was about to hurl.

"Hi."

He looked up and saw Katie coming towards him. "Hi," he said, wiping his palms on his jeans. "Are you busy?"

"I can spare a couple of minutes," she replied, walking around the counter. "What can I do for you?"

The closer she got, the more nervous he became. "The Humane Society this weekend —" He stopped and scratched his head. Why did his tongue get so tangled when he was around her? "This weekend the Humane Society is having a free adoption. I thought maybe..."

She stared at him with her blue eyes.

"Um...I thought that maybe you might want to adopt a cat. And if you do, I could take you there. I mean, if you want me to. It's uh...kind of out of the way..." Realizing he was making a mess of it, he decided to cut his losses and just quit talking.

Katie folded her arms across her. That was absolutely the last thing she'd expected him to say. "I'd like that," she said after a moment.

Relief, coupled with terror, took hold of him, causing his voice to sound funny. "Okay, I'll give you a call."

"Here," she said, pulling her order pad from the pocket of her apron. "Let me give you my number."

Nathan gazed at her as she leaned over the table to write. Her eyelashes were so long, they looked as if they could touch her skin if she closed her eyes.

"Here you go." She handed the paper to him.

"I'll call you Saturday," he said, turning to go.

She gave him a small smile. "That sounds great."

On his way out, he bumped into two chairs.

Chapter Thirteen

Three days later, Nathan sat on the edge of the table in the interrogation room staring at the victims' photos. It had been just over two weeks since Missy Rosenberg's death, yet he took little comfort in the fact that there hadn't been another killing.

He heard the sound of heavy footsteps and looked up.

"You needed me, Boss?"

"Yeah, I need you to check out the owner of the cabins. See if he has an alibi."

Hoskins' mouth twitched as he scratched the side of his neck. "Clayton Hall is about eighty-five years old."

Nathan shook his head. He should have known that. "Okay," he said, stifling a sigh, "see if he has any sons or other relatives that help him run it."

"Will do."

Norma stuck her head in the doorway. "Si? Can you get over to the park? We've gotten several complaints about skateboarders again."

"I'll take care of it, Norma," Nathan said, getting to his feet. "I've got to follow up with something on that side of town anyway."

~

Nathan stepped out of his truck and began making his way up the sidewalk of a small ranch-style brick house. The pavement had cracked in several places, allowing weeds of various heights and shapes to grow through the gaps, while a row of unruly bushes stood on either side of the front door. He felt his stomach tightening as he rang the bell.

The shuffling of feet could be heard, followed by a click. An older man, with wispy gray hair, suddenly appeared. "Chief Sommers."

"Mr. Fuqua, I'm sorry to bother you, but if it's all right, I'd like to ask you a few more questions."

The older man widened the door allowing him to come inside. "I was just about to have some tea. Would you like some?"

"I'd love some." Tea was not one of his favorite drinks, but he didn't want to appear impolite. He followed him into the kitchen and took a seat at a small wooden table.

Nathan glanced around the room as he waited for Mr. Fuqua to join him. Wallpaper with images of flowery bouquets and teapots hung from floor to ceiling, its color having yellowed over time. Above the sink, a set of small copper tins in the shape of roosters hung above the faded wood trim.

The elderly man set the cups down on the table and pulled out his chair.

"Thank you."

"So, what was it you wanted to ask me?"

Nathan cleared his throat as he turned the handle of the mug towards him. "I know we've discussed this previously, but can you be certain that your daughter wasn't seeing anyone?"

The older man picked up his tea and blew the steam off of it. "Not that I was aware of."

"Her co-workers said that she moved in with you about six months ago." Nathan kept his voice gentle, hoping that it would help to soften his words. "Was she having financial troubles?"

"No, no. It was nothing like that," Mr. Fuqua replied, sounding angry. "She was worried about me...she didn't want me living by myself. Her mother died last September." He paused to swallow. "It's been hard."

Nathan rested his hands on the table, allowing a few moments to pass before he spoke again. "When your daughter got off work, did she always come straight home?"

"Usually. Some nights she would go to the grocery or run errands."

"Were there any instances that she didn't come home until late?"

He shrugged. "I guess there were a few, but I didn't really pry into her personal life..." Mr. Fuqua gave him a hurt look. "Carol was a good girl, Chief Sommers. She didn't deserve this."

"No, she didn't."

He brought a wrinkled hand to his forehead. "What kind of person could do that to her? Tying her up like that?" His chin began to tremble as his eyes filled with tears. "I can only imagine how scared she must have been."

Unable to offer him any words of comfort, Nathan shifted his gaze to the table.

Mr. Fuqua lowered his hand and drew an unsteady breath. "I heard that you arrested a guy, but then let him go."

"He was a person of interest, but after questioning him, it was determined that he wasn't the one responsible," he said evenly.

A long sigh fell from the old man's lips.

"I promise we're going to find the person who did this, sir."

Mr. Fuqua wiped at his eyes and gave Nathan a hard look. "That won't make a *damn* bit of difference to my daughter."

~

"Here you go, Chief."

Nathan leaned back, allowing the waitress to set the plate in front of him. "Thank you."

She gave him a nod before looking across the table. "Yours will be out in a minute, Si."

Hoskins smiled sweetly at her. "Thanks, Wanda."

Nathan took a sip of his water, waiting for her to get out of earshot. "What did you find out?"

"Nothin' much. Old man Hall has a grandson that helps him out during the season. His name's Brandon West. No priors and his alibi checks out."

The waitress returned with his plate.

Hoskins removed his elbows from the table as she placed it in front of him. "Thank you, sweetheart."

"It's good to have you back, Si," she said, patting him on his shoulder. "We sure missed you around here."

"It's good to be back."

"You boys need anything else?"

Nathan shook his head. "No, we're good." He watched her move on to the next table before returning his attention to his deputy. Hoskins was in his mid-fifties. He had a crew cut that you could scrape the bottom of your boot on and a hangdog expression that could crack you up. "She's right you know," he said, smiling. "We *did* miss you."

Si shook his head as he picked up his fork. "Not half as much as I missed you guys, believe me. I think if I'd had to stay at home one more day, Sheila would have filed for divorce."

Nathan laughed. "Drivin' her crazy, were you?"

"And then some," he replied, laughing along with him. "Last week, she told me that — "

"Hoskins? What's your 10-20?"

He set his fork down and reached for his mic that was clipped to his epaulet. "I'm at the diner with the chief."

There was a long pause.

"We have a 10-105."

Nathan and Hoskins both pushed their chairs back and stood up.

"What's the location?" Hoskins spoke into the mic as they hurried out.

"Graves Landing."

~

As Nathan and Hoskins rounded the curve, they could see a man standing on the side of the road waving his arms.

"This way," he said, jerking open Nathan's door. "I found her about twenty minutes ago." His breath fell out of him as rapidly as his words.

Nathan slipped out of his seat and caught him by the arm. "Let's talk right here, first. What's your name?"

"Troy Benson. Me and my buddy were fishing near The Shallows when my line got tangled in the brush." He began walking down the embankment. "This way."

Nathan felt his stomach begin to turn as they followed him down the slope. Even from here, he could smell the stench.

Upon reaching the bottom, he saw another man standing about five yards away with a handkerchief covering his mouth and nose. He pointed with his free hand to some tall brush just off the shore.

Nathan unclipped his Glock and handed it to Hoskins before wading into the lake. He began breathing through his mouth instead of his nose to help offset the foul odor that hung in the air.

By the time he reached the edge of the brush, the water was up to his waist. Clenching his jaw, he slowly parted the weeds in front of him and was instantly met by a swarm of flies. The bloated corpse of what appeared to be a young woman lay in the marsh, half-submerged in the mud.

He coughed and gagged as he turned away, the smell and maggots being too much for his stomach to take.

~

Two hours later, Nathan watched as the coroner examined the body. They had moved it up onto the shore a few moments ago. "How long has she been dead?"

"Judging from the deterioration of the body," Jensen said, as he removed the duct tape from her mouth, "I would say about ten or eleven days."

Nathan stood up and walked over to where Hoskins was. He looked at him silently for a moment and then let out a small sigh. "You know what to do."

~

Friday night, Nathan sat alone in his office going over the autopsy report. The girl had been murdered the same as the other four women.

He rested his head against his left hand as he read on. Besides the two small wounds over her heart, she had several bruises and contusions on both of her legs and right arm. Dr. Jensen had also recovered a small amount of tissue from underneath her fingernails. This victim had fought back.

Feeling as if this was their first real break in the case, they had overnighted the sample to the lab in neighboring Custer County with the promise that it would be given priority.

He stared at the girl's name typed at the top of the page. She was currently being called Jane Doe, as no identification had been found on her, or near the crime scene. This had inevitably delayed the autopsy because Jensen refused to perform it until the next of kin had been notified. Nathan had gotten into a shouting match with him over it, giving the nurses in his office an earful. He finally had to resort to asking Manning to step in. Jensen had reluctantly performed it — under protest.

With that obstacle out of the way, he'd set about trying to learn the identity of the girl, but finding out who she was had become a mystery in itself. They had already gone to the cabins and determined that she was not a renter. Norma was checking the surrounding counties for any missing persons that fit her description, but so far, had come up dry.

Nathan looked at the photos that had been taken at the crime scene. The victim's nails had remnants of bright green polish with stickers of tiny stars on them. She was wearing tattered jean shorts and a navy blue sleeveless top. A ragged flip-flop covered her left foot. The other one had been found floating near the bank about a hundred yards away. She appeared younger than the other victims, although, with the decomposition, he couldn't be sure.

The more he studied her, the more he began to wonder if she was a runaway. If she were, he knew from experience that the probability that anyone was looking for her was fairly small — making her an easy target. In the majority of cases involving older teens, the homes they had left behind usually held an abusive parent or step-parent, the nature of which was usually sexual.

"Nathan?"

He looked up to find Katie standing in the doorway.

She gave him a small smile and then glanced behind her. "Where is everyone?"

He pushed his chair back and stood up. "They've gone home for the night," he said quietly.

Her eyes went from him to the file lying open on his desk. "I heard about the girl. It must be hard."

He closed the folder and nodded, hearing the sincerity in her voice.

"I wanted to stop by and tell you that it's okay if you can't come with me tomorrow. I understand that this takes precedence."

"That's very kind of you," he said, trying to cover the fact that he'd completely forgotten. "But I think I can spare a couple of hours in the morning."

The smile returned to her face, highlighting the beauty of it. "I'll see you tomorrow, then."

Nathan glanced out the window and saw that it was getting dark. "Let me walk you to your car."

"That's all right," she said, shaking her head.

"No, wait."

Something in his voice made her stop and turn around.

He grabbed his keys from off the desk and pulled the door to his office closed.

She waited patiently for him to lock up the station before starting down the steps.

Nathan remained silent as he escorted her across the street.

Upon reaching her car, she gave him a small smile. "Thanks."

"I'll pick you up around eight in the morning. Is that okay?"

She started to answer him but saw that his attention was not on her. His eyes were rapidly searching up and down the block. "That's fine," she replied, although she was fairly certain he hadn't heard her.

He nodded absently. "Be careful driving home."

~

Cheryl came home and threw her purse down on the kitchen table. She closed her eyes and smiled as the air conditioner greeted her like an old friend. Leaning against the counter for balance, she kicked off her shoes and wiggled her toes, allowing them to breathe.

She'd had to run the register this afternoon as one of her employees had called in sick. She didn't mind doing it, but it had left her with no time to work on next month's schedule or sign off on the time cards.

She tilted her head back and let it roll around her shoulders, trying to ease the ache in her neck. It used to be that she enjoyed being the general manager, and eagerly tackled all the responsibilities that went along with it. But this baby was literally sucking the life out of her, making things like time cards and paperwork annoying.

As she raised her head up, she noticed how quiet it was in the house. "Jack?"

"In here," he called out.

She passed through the living room and went down the hall before coming to a stop outside the nursery. Jack was sitting on the floor with pieces of the crib scattered all around him.

He looked up from the instructions he was reading. "How was work?"

She plopped herself down in the rocking chair next to the window and sighed. "Long. I am *so* glad to be home."

He went back to reading the instructions.

Cheryl watched him reach for a long piece of the painted wood. He turned it this way, that way, and then over, before scratching his head and peering at the paper again. She suppressed a smile. Her husband was not the most mechanically inclined. "You know you don't have to do this tonight."

He flipped a page back. "I know. But I've been promising you all week I'd do it. Tonight seemed like a good night."

"Why don't you just let Nathan help you?" she asked, pressing her back into the cushion.

"I really don't want to do that," he said, reaching for his screwdriver.

"Why not? He said that he'd be glad to help."

A sigh fell from his lips as he sorted through a bag of screws. "Because."

"Because why?"

Jack let the screwdriver fall from his hand as he jerked his head towards her. "Because he's really having a hard time with this, Cheryl. I don't want to throw it in his face."

She looked out the window, feeling both hurt and embarrassed.

"Sorry," he said after a moment.

"It's all right. I know you've got a lot on your mind." But the truth was, he'd been in a bad mood since yesterday.

"Well," he said, crawling over to where she sat. "I didn't mean to take it out on you." He pressed his lips against hers, and then bent down to kiss her swollen stomach.

Cheryl could feel his tension slipping away as she ran her fingers through his hair. "What's in the bag?" she asked, noticing a small paper sack sitting on the floor beside her foot.

He raised his head and smiled. "I got this for the baby today." He opened it up and pulled out a tiny red-and-white jersey. Billings Mustangs was printed on the front of it.

Cheryl resisted the urge to giggle as she took it from him.

"Do you think she'll like it?"

She leaned forward and kissed him on his forehead. "She's going to love it."

Chapter Fourteen

The next morning, Katie noticed Nathan's mood had improved somewhat as he drove her to the animal shelter. At least he was carrying on a conversation with her, which was more than the last time they had been together in a vehicle.

"Do you want a male or female?" he asked as they traveled along a gravel road filled with potholes.

"Mmm, I'm not sure. I guess it really doesn't matter."

He slowed down and turned into a small parking lot. A long building covered in white siding sat near the back of it.

Nathan got out and walked around the front of his truck to open the door for her.

"Thank you." As she slid from the seat, she gave him a sideways glance. He was wearing faded jeans and a dark t-shirt that complimented the color of his eyes.

He gave her an awkward smile. "You're welcome."

The gravel crunched underneath her sandals as she began making her way towards the entrance.

Upon stepping inside, they were immediately greeted by the sound of barking dogs, and a smell that made Katie wrinkle her nose.

A little girl, who appeared to be about nine, walked past them with her mother. She was proudly toting a small yellow kitten in her arms.

Nathan bent down and smiled. "Is this your kitty?"

The girl smiled shyly at him. "Yes."

"What's its name?" he asked, scratching it between the ears.

She tightened her grip as it wiggled. "I think I'm going to call him Tiger."

He grinned as he straightened up and held the door open for them. "Take good care of him."

"I will."

The mother nodded at him. "How are you doing, Nathan?"

"I'm good." He gestured towards the little girl. "I can't believe how big she's gotten."

She arched her eyebrows. "She's ten going on twenty."

He gave a small laugh. "It was good seeing you."

"You too."

An older woman with brown frazzled hair and a worn appearance approached Katie. "Can I help you?"

Nathan turned away from the door. "This young lady is looking to adopt a cat."

The woman gestured with her hand. "Follow me." She had a hurried, worried walk about her as she led them towards the back.

Katie couldn't help noticing that the shrill barks had gotten louder and that the smell had grown more pungent. It made her want to turn around and go back outside.

"These are the cats we have available for open adoption," she said, pointing to the row of pens on the left.

Katie held her breath as she and Nathan began making their way down the aisle. Each pen held at least two cats. She took her time, stopping to look at each one, but soon found herself wishing she could care for all of them. The fact that they were here didn't bother her nearly as much as the reason *why* they were here; nobody wanted them.

She suddenly felt Nathan's hand on the small of her back.

"Are you all right?" he asked in a gentle voice.

"Yeah," she answered, pushing her thoughts to the side. "It's just the smell."

He made a face. "It's pretty bad, isn't it?"

They continued walking down the row. Up ahead in the last pen, she saw a small black-and-white paw reaching out for her. She stopped and bent down to get a closer look. "Hi there," she whispered, poking her finger through the wire.

The cat, starved for attention, began rubbing its chin hard against the tip of her fingernail.

Nathan knelt beside her. "He's cute."

She nodded in agreement. This cat had the longest whiskers of any she'd ever seen before.

They looked as if she could tie them in a bow. "I like him."

Nathan looked over his shoulder. "Marge? Can we see this one?"

"Sure thing, Chief," she said, stepping between them to unlock the pen. "This one is a male."

Katie gathered him into her arms and began to stroke his matted fur, eliciting a deep purr from his throat.

"What do you think?"

She glanced up and saw that Nathan was leaning against the pen, smiling. She felt her cheeks flush as she smiled back. "I'll take him."

~

The cat did not like riding in the truck. Katie tried to hold him, but he was having none of it.

It climbed up the seats, hid under the seats, climbed up Nathan's arm, slid down Nathan's arm—and cried the entire way home.

Nathan pulled into the driveway and abruptly shifted the gear into park. "Come here, cat," he said, reaching between his legs. He dragged him out from underneath the seat and held him against his chest before opening the door.

Katie hurried across the yard and up her front steps. "Can you bring him into the kitchen for me?" she asked, sliding her key into the lock. "I just want to give him something to eat. Maybe it will calm him down."

"Sure." Nathan tucked him under his arm like a football and followed her inside.

"Meow!" he cried pathetically as he struggled to get down.

Nathan waited for her to pour a generous helping of food into the dish before turning him loose.

The cat hunkered down for a moment as he looked at his surroundings. Upon spying the food, he slunk over, with his belly low to the ground, and began devouring it.

"So, what are you going to name him?"

"I have no idea," she replied, straightening up. "I'll have to think about it."

The walkie-talkie he had clipped to his belt began to have some chatter on it. Nathan listened for a moment and then reached behind him to turn it down.

As he did, Katie noticed two long scratches on the side of his forearm. "Oh, Nathan. I'm so sorry he did that to you."

He glanced down at his arm and shrugged. "It's all right."

She wet a paper towel and pressed it against the scratches. As she began wiping away the blood, she couldn't help noticing how tall he was. Her head barely reached the tops of his shoulders. When she was finished, she laid her hand on his wrist and looked up at him. "Would you like a Band-Aid?"

Katie's sudden touch stimulated the hair on his arms, making them stand at attention. He smiled down at her. "No, I'm fine."

"Chief, do you copy?"

He unclipped the radio from his belt and brought it to his lips. "This is the chief. Go ahead."

"There's a 10-55 at the corner of Fourth and Lexington."

"I'm on my way."

"10-4."

He clipped the radio back to his belt. "Sorry, I need to go."

"What's a 10-55?" Katie asked, walking him to the door.

"Traffic accident."

"Thank you for taking me to get my cat."

"You're welcome." As they went into the living room, he gestured at the cans of paint stacked in the corner. "Looks like you're going to be busy."

"I was hoping to be able to get some painting done today."

He tilted his head and laughed. "That sounds like *zero* fun."

"I know, I know, but I'm not planning on working the rest of the weekend, and I'd like to get at least one room painted and decorated before Monday."

"Well," he said, opening the door, "have fun with that."

She stood on the step as he hurried towards his truck. "Nathan?"

He stopped and turned.

"If you finish your work early, you can give me a call. Maybe we can have lunch or dinner..." She let her voice trail off, uncertain if it was the intense heat or her words that was causing a pinkish hue to encircle his cheeks.

"All right." He gave her an awkward nod and slid behind the wheel.

~

By the time Nathan got to Graves Landing, it was almost noon. Jack was already down there combing through the area.

He ducked under the crime scene tape and made his way towards the shore. The girl's body had been found in a small peninsula known as The Shallows. The water in this area was only about four feet deep, yet was laden with tall grass and heavy brush, making it resemble a small marsh.

"Morning, Nathan."

"Jack," he replied. "Got anything?"

He squinted into the sun and shook his head. "Nothing yet. Norma's still checking with missing persons, but hasn't come across anything."

The sound of a Jet Ski made them turn. Two boys raced across the water as they cut around the peninsula.

"Have you heard anything back from the lab?" asked Nathan.

"I'm still waiting for them to return my call."

"Where's Hoskins?"

"He's down at the docks showing the victim's picture around."

Nathan sighed. The picture Jack was referring to had been taken as she lay on a slab at the morgue. He hated showing a photo of a dead girl to the people around town, but unfortunately, it was all they had.

~

It was late afternoon when they finished searching the area, and to Nathan's utter disappointment, they had turned up nothing. He lifted the bottom of his t-shirt and wiped the sweat from his face. "You ready to head back?"

"Yeah," Jack answered.

As the two of them made their way up the slope, the distinct sound of a car coming to a stop could be heard.

After a moment, Nathan saw Tom Manning peering down. Even from here he could see the anger in his face.

"Mayor," Nathan said as he reached the top.

"Nathan. Collins." He gave them a curt nod.

Jack nodded back and then walked over to his truck.

Manning waited until he'd gotten out of earshot before speaking. "What have you found?"

Nathan shook his head. "Nothing yet."

"*Goddamn it*, Nathan! How many more women is this guy going to kill before you catch him?"

Jack watched silently as the mayor tore into his former son-in-law. He turned around and leaned against the grill of his truck, embarrassed for Nathan.

"Collins, do you read me?"

He fingered the button on his mic. "Go ahead, Si."

"A local recognized the girl. Says she went to high school here. I'm on my way to the principal's house now to check on it."

"All right. I'll tell the chief." He let go of the button and ran his hand through his damp hair. He could still hear the mayor yelling. It wasn't long before Nathan raised his voice as well, turning it into a full-fledged argument.

Jack was aware of the close relationship Jenny had with her father, and he knew that he grieved for her as badly as Nathan did. In fact, it was hard to look at either man and not think of her. The two of them were bound by circumstance.

Manning spouted a few more choice words before getting in his car and driving away, his tires slinging dirt and rocks as he peeled out.

Jack hung back, trying to give Nathan some breathing room. He allowed a few minutes to pass before he turned and walked over to where he was standing. "We may have an I.D. on the victim," he said softly. "Hoskins is checking it out now."

Nathan opened the back of his truck and pulled out two bottles of water from a small cooler. The vehicle was parked in a shady spot, providing a much-needed relief to the two of them as they sat on the tailgate.

"The mayor sure was in a snit," Jack said, twisting off the cap.

"He's *always* in a snit." Nathan smiled slightly, pretending that he was unscathed by his former father-in-law's remarks.

They sat in silence waiting for Hoskins to call.

"Have you decided on a name yet?" Nathan's voice came out quieter than he'd intended.

Jack took a long sip of water before answering. "Lydia Marie."

"That's nice."

"Yeah." Jack shrugged as he swatted away a wasp. *God*, he wished Hoskins would call. "Would you mind if I cut out early today?"

Nathan finished his water and tossed it in the back of his truck. "Nope. You have plans for this evening?"

Jack rubbed the back of his neck, embarrassed to answer. "It's our anniversary."

Nathan shook his head. It was something he should have remembered.

It was the twenty-first of June, and the rain that had been forecasted for this afternoon had yet to appear. The clouds instead, had given way to a very beautiful, albeit, warm day.

Nathan wiped a bead of sweat from the side of his face as he stood at the altar waiting for the ceremony to begin. Jack stood next to him fidgeting with one of his cuffs. He couldn't remember a time when he'd seen him so nervous.

After what seemed like an eternity, the music finally began to play, and the murmurs from the crowd died down. Nathan solemnly watched as Cheryl's sister began making her way down the aisle. Jenny should have been right here, at this moment, walking towards him. She was supposed to have been Cheryl's maid of honor.

He saw Jack casually watching him out of the corner of his eye as if he knew what he was thinking. He was probably worried that he was going to break down. Nathan held his head up high and took a deep breath. Not today. Not today, because he had consumed several ounces of vodka before coming here. It was the only way he was going to get through this.

The wedding march began to play and Nathan watched as Jack's bride appeared. She had her arm locked tightly onto her father's as he escorted her down the aisle.

Cheryl looked radiant, like an angel all dressed in white. A beautiful smile, beautiful face, beautiful personality.

Jack stood in awe as she drew near.

The ceremony itself was nothing but a blur. Nathan remembered handing Jack the ring, but only heard bits and pieces of what the minister had said.

Afterwards, he posed with the wedding party for the countless pictures that had to be taken. He stood where the photographer placed him and smiled when he was told to.

~

A low rumble of thunder sounded in the distance as dark clouds began rolling in.

Nathan sat alone, quietly sipping his champagne. The pictures had all been taken, the cake had been cut, and the happy couple was now sharing their first dance.

He watched them swaying back and forth on the portable wooden floor. Jack's fingers were intertwined with Cheryl's as their bodies pressed close to one another. He was whispering something into her ear and smiling.

"How are you, Nathan?"

He immediately recognized the voice behind him and quickly got to his feet — a little too quickly apparently, as he stumbled backward.

A gentle hand reached out to steady him.

He pulled himself out of its grasp and gripped the back of the chair.

"How have you been, Nathan?" she asked in a silky voice. Her long raven hair gathered around her sun-kissed shoulders while the tight black dress she was wearing accented every curve she had.

"How do you think?" he asked, glancing around uneasily.

Her dark-brown eyes swept across the dance floor and surrounding tables. "There's no one watching us."

Feeling as if he were suffocating, he reached up and unbuttoned his collar.

"I just wanted to tell you how sorry I was about your wife, and — "

"Thanks." Anger began to simmer inside him.

"Nathan..."

"I can't see you anymore," he said in a low voice.

"I know." She reached out and touched his hand, letting her fingers caress the back of it.

Nathan's breath suddenly rushed out of him.

"Take care of yourself."

The wind began to pick up as he watched her walking away. He couldn't help but notice Jack watching her as well as he danced with Cheryl.

He loosened his tie and sat back down in his chair, his fingers grasping for the glass of champagne. He tilted his head back, letting the liquid spill down his throat. When he was finished, he saw the bride and groom heading his way.

"Come on, Nathan," Cheryl said, holding out her hands. "Dance with me."

He shook his head politely. "I'm not a very good dancer."

Cheryl reached for his arm and pulled, refusing to take no for an answer. "Oh, come on!"

He managed to get to his feet. "It's getting late. I've got an early day tomorrow."

"What are you doing tomorrow?"

Nathan turned his attention to Jack, who was staring at the empty champagne glasses strewn about the table. "Well," he said, fumbling inside his coat pocket, "somebody's got to cover the station while you two go on your honeymoon."

Jack suddenly looked up.

"Here," said Nathan, holding an envelope out to him.

He hesitantly took it and peered inside. "It's for a bed and breakfast in Miles City..." He began shaking his head. "Nathan, I don't know what to say."

"Don't say anything. Just have a great time."

Cheryl's eyes brimmed with tears as she stepped forward to hug him. "Thank you, Nathan."

"You're welcome."

"Come on, Jack!" Cheryl laughed as she grabbed his hand. "We've got some packing to do!"

"I'll be right there," he said, smiling.

The two men watched as she hurried over to some of the guests to show them.

"This was really nice of you."

Nathan shifted his gaze back to him. "Well, I couldn't let you spend your honeymoon working. Honeymoons are meant for...well...honeymooning."

"Does this mean you're staying?"

"For now," he answered quietly.

~

Small spatters of rain started to fall as Nathan walked through the park towards his truck. The few guests that remained began saying their goodbyes as the drops got bigger.

He fished in his pocket for his keys as he neared the street, but his steps faltered when he saw Mac Hodges leaning against his truck. He felt his jaw tighten. He had not seen him since the day before the accident.

"I've been waiting for you, Chief."

Nathan disliked the way he said that word. He always made it sound condescending. "What do you want, Hodges?"

"What I want is irrelevant, now," he replied in a voice laced with bitterness.

Choosing to ignore him, Nathan unlocked his door.

Hodges suddenly grabbed his arm and turned him to face him. "She was mine! When she left Silver Creek, she promised that she would come home to me!"

Nathan jerked his arm free, trying to keep a lid on his temper. There was nothing he would've liked more than to pound him six feet into the earth, but he was not about to ruin Cheryl's day. He knew she had already shed enough tears.

"All of this," Hodges continued, "all of this is your fault!"

Nathan bowed his head as he braced his arms against the door of his truck. He was silent for a long time. When he spoke, his voice shook. "You should have come to me first, Mac. You never should have sent her those pictures."

He set his champagne glass on the hood of Nathan's truck and took a step closer. "Well, I guess that's something I'm just gonna have to live with. But what about you, Chief? Can you live with what you've done?"

A blinding rage tore through him as he grabbed Hodges by his shirt and shoved him to the ground. He immediately straddled him and raised his fist, but before he could slam it into Mac's face, someone caught him around the arm and jerked him to his feet.

"That's enough!" Jack pushed him up against the fender of his truck.

"About time you got here."

Jack turned his attention to Hodges. "You need to go home, Mac," he said, helping him to his feet.

"Why are you taking his side? I'm the one that got assaulted."

"I didn't see anything."

Mac sighed and shook his head. "Of course you didn't."

"Go home," Jack repeated.

Hodges brushed his pants off and gave Nathan a sideways glance as he turned away. "See ya around, Chief."

Nathan took a step forward, but Jack held him back, refusing to let him go until Hodges had made it across the street.

"What was that all about?"

Nathan reached out and knocked the champagne glass off his truck. "Nothing."

"It didn't look like nothing."

"He's drunk," he said, jerking open his door.

"So are you."

Nathan looked at him for a moment before sliding into the seat and starting the engine.

"Let me get Hoskins to drive you home."

"I'll drive slow," he said, putting it into gear. He glanced over at his deputy and forced a smile. "Have a nice honeymoon."

A burst of static came over the radio drawing Nathan back.

"Collins?"

"Go ahead, Si," Jack said into his mic.

"The principal made a positive I.D. on the victim."

~

Nathan drove down Wilson Boulevard looking for apartment 809E. Upon spotting the building, he pulled in behind a beat-up Buick that had seen better days.

Several boys, trying to act older than they were, watched him from across the street as he got out of his truck.

The Wilson Housing Projects was well known for its meth problem. Nathan had made several arrests here over the past few months and was not very popular among the tenants. As he absorbed the harsh looks being thrown his way, he knew that questioning them would be pointless. This was a tight-lipped community that would just as soon put up with their neighbor dealing drugs, rather than turn him in.

He stepped over a tricycle with a missing wheel as he made his way up the sidewalk. Seeing that the door was open, he rapped loudly on the screen in order to be heard over the television that was blaring inside.

A blond-haired boy in a sagging diaper and juice stained t-shirt greeted him.

"Hi there," Nathan said, smiling down at him.

The boy grinned back.

A woman suddenly stepped in front of him. "What do you want?" Her tone of voice was neither kind nor angry—just indifferent.

He held up his badge. "I'm Nathan Sommers, Chief of Police. I need to know if a Marissa Thomas lives here."

"Yeah, she lives here," she answered, picking the boy up. "What's she done?"

"Would it be all right if I came in for a moment?"

A look of dismay came across her as she unlocked the screen door and held it open for him.

"Thank you." He stopped in the entranceway when he realized she wasn't going to let him come in any further.

"Is Marissa in trouble?" Again, there was only indifference in her voice.

"Are you her mother?"

"Grandmother. She lives with me," she said, snapping off the television.

"When was the last time you saw your granddaughter, ma'am?"

She put the boy on the floor and pulled a pack of cigarettes out. "I don't know. She's come and gone all summer long." She lit the cigarette and put it to her lips.

Nathan watched as she drew the smoke into her lungs. Her cheeks sank inwards, revealing the deep crevices in her face. "Does Marissa have a boyfriend? Or do you know any of her friends —"

"Look, I ain't got *time* to keep up with her social life! Just tell me what she's done!"

Nathan glanced down at the boy for a moment, steeling himself for what he had to say. "I'm sorry, but Marissa's body was found in the lake Thursday afternoon. Someone murdered her."

~

Jack closed his eyes and breathed deeply as Cheryl's fingers worked out the knots in his shoulders. "You have the touch of an angel."

She smiled to herself as her hands dug harder into the muscles under his skin. He had gotten home about an hour ago and she could tell by his silence that it had not been a good day.

A friend of hers from work had shown her several sites on the internet that had posted articles about the killings. Along with the gruesome details, the victims' pictures were also displayed. She couldn't help noticing that Mac Hodges was the contributing editor on nearly all of them.

The man was already causing a great deal of tension with his articles in the Prairie County Gazette. Every Sunday, for the past month, the headlines had been about the murders. She couldn't deny it was newsworthy, but she didn't like the fact that he took the opportunity to insinuate that the police department was incompetent. And now, he had taken his slander global.

"Cheryl?"

"What?"

Jack was staring at her over his shoulder. "Did you hear me?"

"Sorry," she replied, pushing her thoughts to the side.

"What did Jensen say when you saw him this morning?"

"That I'm two centimeters dilated."

"So, what does that mean exactly?" he asked, turning around on the bed to face her.

She smiled softly at him. "It means that it won't be much longer."

Jack's face grew pale.

"Are you okay, sweetheart?"

"Yeah," he said, moving his hand to her belly.

She lay back against the pillow and watched as he caressed her bump. "You know, I can't even see my feet," she lamented.

"Well, *I* can see them," he said, looking down at her toes, "and they're *very* sexy."

She laughed. "That's because they're the only part of my body that's not huge."

"I think *everything* about you is sexy," he said, bending down to kiss her.

Cheryl closed her eyes as his lips lingered there, longing to do more. She lightly slid her tongue over them, telling him it was all right.

Jack stretched out beside her and began moving his mouth along the side of her neck and throat. She felt the backs of his fingers as they stroked her thighs; starting at the knee, they ran all the way up to the bottom of her panties.

After a moment, he slipped his fingers inside and slowly slid them down. He pushed her sundress over her stomach and kissed her just below her pelvis.

She breathed in deeply as his tongue began circling her. Her legs instinctively parted, allowing him to roam free. She arched her back and moaned as she clumsily felt for his zipper.

Jack got to his knees and unbuckled his pants.

She jerked them down and slid her hands around his bare skin. His flesh was hot against hers as he pushed inside. He was careful to keep his weight off of her as he gently glided up and down, taking his time.

Her body began to tingle all over. She didn't know if it was because it had been so long, or the fact that he was going so slow, but her feelings came hard and fast. She trembled beneath him as a soft cry escaped her lips.

Jack's breath jerked out of him as he pressed his cheek against hers. After a moment, he raised himself up and looked into her eyes. "Did I hurt you?"

"No," she said, touched by his genuine concern for her and the baby.

He withdrew and put his head down on the pillow beside her. "Do you know how much I love you?"

"How much?"

"To the ends of the earth and back again."

Cheryl smiled as she snuggled up against him. The first time he'd ever told her that was the night he'd proposed.

He interlocked his fingers with hers and drew them to his lips. "You are the best thing that ever happened to me."

She looked at her hand, admiring the mother's ring he'd given her earlier. The dark-red ruby sparkled in the fading sunlight.

"Do you like it?"

"I love it," she said, propping her chin upon his chest. "It's beautiful."

He smiled as he brushed her hair from her shoulders. "So, where can I take you to eat for our anniversary?"

A contented sigh fell from her. "How about if we just order a pizza?"

"A pizza, huh?"

"It's too hot to go out, and I'm really comfortable right now."

"Do you want *Mario's* or *Guido's?*"

"*Mario's.* There's a coupon on the fridge."

He zipped his pants up and kissed her on the forehead. "I'll be right back."

As he left the room, Cheryl noticed a folded piece of paper lying on the covers beside her. Guessing it must have fallen out of his pocket, she started to put it on the nightstand, but stopped when she saw the face of a young girl.

An involuntary shudder went down her spine, causing her shoulders to shake. Everything about these murders was unsettling. It was like a dark force had descended upon them. A force that no one could see, or hear, yet had taken five lives.

And it was poised to come again and again, until it decided to move on, or was caught.

She turned the paper over and placed it on the nightstand. Her emotions began to surge just as Jack walked back into the room. Feeling the onslaught of tears, she looked away.

"What's wrong?"

"I really don't know," she lied as she wiped at her eyes.

He wrapped his arms tightly around her and kissed her on the cheek. "I know you're nervous about having the baby, but everything's going to be all right, sweetheart."

She laid her head upon his shoulder as the tears rolled down her face. She had a horrible feeling that nothing was going to be right ever again.

Chapter Fifteen

Nathan felt his anger churning as he stared at the newspaper headlines. '*The Monster of Silver Creek Claims Fifth Victim*'. The photo accompanying the article showed a body bag being lifted onto a stretcher.

Hodges had written an in-depth piece about the string of murders. The names of the women, along with their backgrounds, had been printed in the order that they'd been killed. It stated that, as of press time, the fifth victim still remained unidentified. Folding the paper in half, he chucked it into the wastebasket.

He opened Marissa Thomas' folder and stared at her picture for a long time. Now that he knew her identity, her death seemed even more senseless than it had before. A background check revealed that she'd been arrested twice in the past nine months for possession.

Nathan closed the file — and his eyes. Having just turned eighteen, this girl had lived a hard life and had never gotten the opportunity to know a better one. The only thing she would be remembered for was being the fifth victim of a serial killer.

~

Katie stood in the middle of her small garage surveying the vast assortment of boxes. She had hoped that today would be the day that she would finally be able to get her car inside, but her enthusiasm had immediately waned the minute she'd stepped into the sweltering heat.

Nearly all of the cardboard boxes in her midst were unmarked, meaning that she had absolutely no clue what was inside of them. Pressing forward, she tore open the first one thinking she might get lucky and find her missing pots and pans. She didn't. As she opened box after box, it only made her realize that she had accumulated a lot of junk.

The sound of an engine made her look up. Nathan's truck was pulling into her driveway. She quickly finger-combed her hair while simultaneously wiping the sweat off her face.

"This doesn't look like any fun," he said, walking inside the garage.

She put her hands on her hips and smiled. "Well, I have to agree with you on that."

He stopped on the other side of the box she was going through. "I came by to see how you and your cat were getting along."

"We're doing fine. Would you like to come in and see for yourself?"

"I don't want to bother you."

"Oh, please. You're doing me a favor," she said, heading up the steps. "I'm tired of looking at boxes."

The door to the garage led to a small laundry room. "Sorry," she said, moving a pile of clothes out of the way with her foot. "Just walk around those."

As Nathan followed her into the living room, he immediately noticed the transformation. The walls had gone from a dingy white to a soothing sage green overnight. "The room looks great."

A satisfactory smile formed on her lips. "It took me most of yesterday, but I'm really happy with how it turned out."

As she sat down on the sofa, she noticed he was wearing his gun and badge. "Are you on duty today?"

"I'm always on duty," he answered, sitting down next to her. "It's one of the drawbacks of being the chief."

"Meow…"

Katie shifted her attention to the floor and smiled. "Come here, Lance."

Nathan arched his eyebrow. "Lance?"

"Yeah. He looks like a Lance to me."

A second later, the cat jumped up in her lap.

"Well, hi there," he said, reaching out to pet him.

Katie studied the scratches on Nathan's forearm. They were each about five inches long and had scabbed over. "I'm very sorry about those."

He shook his head. "They're not fatal. I won't have to be put down."

"Well," she said, laughing, "if you start frothing at the mouth, I may have to call animal control."

He smiled nervously, trying to remember all the conversation starters he had gone over in his head during the drive over. "Oh." He leaned back and reached into his front pocket. "I brought something for him."

"You did?"

"Mmm-hmm." He handed her a small package containing a fuzzy blue mouse.

"Thank you, Nathan. That was very sweet of you."

"You're welcome," he mumbled, suddenly feeling embarrassed.

She opened the plastic package and dangled the mouse by its squiggly tail. "Here, Lance. What do you think?"

Lance sniffed the mouse inquisitively and then hopped down.

"I'm sure he'll play with it later," she said, smiling.

The room grew still, causing Nathan to tense. His conversation starters had all left his mind, making him draw a blank.

After an awkward silence, Katie spoke first. "Would you like to stay for lunch? I can make us some sandwiches."

"I'd love to."

"Well, then," she said, standing up. "Let's go to the kitchen."

Nathan leaned against the counter as he watched her reach into the fridge. She pulled out a bag of sliced turkey and then got out an armload of condiments. It was like watching an artist at work. She skillfully spread mayo and mustard on the slices of bread before layering it with turkey and cheese.

She held up a small jar. "Do you like horseradish?"

"Sure."

Her fingers nimbly sliced a tomato and placed it in the center before topping it with another piece of bread. Grabbing a long knife, she started to cut it crossways.

"Well, I was going to ask you if I could help, but I think I would just get in your way."

She began to giggle as she cut the other sandwich.

It was a sweet giggle, and Nathan liked the way her nose crinkled when she did it. He took the plates from her and placed them on the table in front of a large bay window.

Katie handed him a glass of ice water and sat down across from him.

"This looks great," he said, taking a large bite. Flavor immediately began to fill his mouth. "It's very good."

"Thank you," she replied, before taking a bite of her own sandwich.

"So, how are things at the bakery?"

"Pretty good," she said, after swallowing. "I'm starting to get some regular customers."

"My deputy wouldn't happen to be one of them, would he?"

She laughed as she wiped her mouth. "I plead the fifth."

Lance hopped up on the chair beside Nathan and pawed at his hand.

"What's this?"

Katie shook her head. "He's not shy about begging for food." She watched as he tore off a little piece of turkey and fed it to him. "Do you like being the chief of police?"

"It's okay," he answered, watching Lance devour the turkey.

"I read the article about the murders in today's paper. It must be hard dealing with all that."

"Which are you referring to? The paper, or the murders?"

"Both, I guess," she answered, finding his question strange.

He took another bite of his sandwich.

"How long have you been the chief?"

"About four years now."

Lance pawed incessantly at his hand again.

Nathan looked down at him. "Don't you think you've had enough?" He fed him another piece.

She watched him silently as he took a sip of his water. "Cheryl told me that you used to be a detective in Sacramento."

His face suddenly flushed. "What else did Cheryl tell you about me?"

Katie blinked, surprised by his tone.

He set his glass down and looked at her expectantly.

She knew he was waiting for her to say it.

Nathan turned his head towards the window, his jaw clenched. Cheryl had no right.

A moment later, he felt her hand upon his forearm.

"Nathan?"

He shifted his gaze back to her. Her blue eyes were fixed intently upon him.

"Please don't be mad. She thought it would be easier on you if I already knew."

He felt his anger rising and swallowed hard. He recognized the sympathetic look she was giving him. It was something that he had grown to resent from the people in this town.

As she watched him trying to control his feelings, it became apparent to her just how emotionally raw he still was. "I'm sorry," she whispered.

Nathan cleared his throat. "You know, you should really get some blinds up. People can see in here at night."

Katie's eyes went from him to the window. "I've got some," she said, letting go of his arm. "I just haven't been able to get them hung."

~

That evening, Katie lay soaking in her bathtub. She had been in here so long that the tips of her fingers had wrinkled, but she was too comfortable to move.

Lance sat watching her from his perch on the toilet seat. His eyes were big and green, and at times appeared opalescent. Except for the white on his chest and feet, his fur was a shiny black. He looked like he was wearing an ascot and little booties.

She leaned her head against the back of the tub and closed her eyes. All things considering, it had been a nice weekend. She'd gotten her living room painted and fixed the way she'd wanted, and had procured the boy down the street to start cutting her grass.

Unfortunately, her car still sat outside the garage, but she promised herself that she would work on it tomorrow evening.

Nathan had stayed for most of the afternoon helping her hang blinds and curtains. He seemed to quickly dismiss what had happened at lunch, giving her the impression that he was very good at pretending.

She sank further into the water, letting it lap at her chin. He was an odd duck. Cheryl had all but told her as much, but she didn't quite understand what she meant until today.

~

Nathan stared into his empty refrigerator. Still angry with Cheryl for telling Katie what had happened, he'd decided to skip dinner at the Collins' household tonight. Starting a relationship based on pity was not what he wanted.

Deciding he was more tired than hungry, he made his way into the bathroom to wash his face and get ready for bed. As he waited for the water to get hot, he studied his reflection in the mirror. He began to wonder what it was that Katie saw in him, or if she saw anything at *all*. There was certainly nothing redeeming about himself that he could think of.

The cool March wind blew through the open window causing the sheers to flutter softly against the sill. Nathan lay in the darkness holding a stranger in his arms. A woman whom he'd only met the day before. He suddenly sat up and swung his legs over the side of her bed. His face was hot and flushed as he reached up to wipe the sweat away.

He felt her fingertips gliding along his back and sighed. A few moments ago, her touch had excited him to no end. Now he just found it irritating. Overwhelmed by guilt, he bowed his head.

"What's the matter, Nathan?"

He clenched his jaw, unable to answer.

"Are you worried about your wife?"

"This was a mistake," he finally said.

She slid her hands around to the front of his chest and kissed the side of his neck. "It's only a mistake if you allow it to be one."

He looked at her over his shoulder. "I've allowed it to happen. I never should have come here."

"Do you love her?"

He closed his eyes as a rush of angst tore through him.

Nathan struck out at the mirror with his fist, cracking his reflection on impact. He gripped the edge of the vanity as he shook with anger. There had been no reason for him to sleep with her. No reason at all.

He watched the bright red blood seep from his knuckles and trickle into the sink. All he had to do was walk away. But he hadn't. He had gone over there knowing exactly what was going to take place, and he had done so willingly — time and time again.

Chapter Sixteen

Monday morning, an unkempt and unshaven Nathan, straggled into the station house.

"Morning, Chief."

He nodded at his employees as he made his way over to the coffee machine.

"What happened?" asked Jack, gesturing at the bandage on his right hand.

"I cut it last night."

He waited for more information, but after a moment, it became clear that there would be none forthcoming.

An awkward silence fell across the room as Norma and Hoskins exchanged glances.

Jack cleared his throat and reached into his shirt pocket. "Here you go, Norma. Cheryl wanted me to be sure and give you an invitation."

"I'll be there," she said with a smile. "I just love baby showers."

"Where's mine?" asked Hoskins.

Norma set the card on her desk and rolled her eyes. "It's a baby shower, Si. It's for *women*."

"Aren't you gonna be there, Collins?"

Jack shook his head and laughed. "Absolutely not."

"I've got him working that day," Nathan said, walking over to join in on the conversation.

"Thanks," Jack replied.

Nathan took a sip of his coffee and laughed. "It's the *very* least I could do."

The bell above the door chimed and they turned to see a young girl hesitantly walking towards them. She was wearing a black t-shirt, jean shorts, and tattered sandals.

"Good morning." Hoskins got up from his chair and offered her a smile as broad as his shoulders. "How can we help you?"

She clutched at her purse strap as her eyes darted nervously around the station house, eventually coming to rest upon Jack. "I need to speak with you."

Finding the seriousness in her voice a little unsettling, Jack set his mug on the desk and stood up. "Let's go back here where we can talk in private," he said, extending his arm.

She nodded and started towards the interrogation room.

Jack looked at Nathan and shrugged before turning to follow.

The girl walked into the room and stopped abruptly, causing Jack to have to take a large step to the left in order to avoid bumping into the back of her.

"Please, have a seat," he said, pulling out a chair.

Her hands still clutched at her purse strap as she sat down.

"Would you like some coffee, or anything to drink?"

She shook her head.

As he sat down across from her, she locked eyes with him once more. "Do I know you?" he asked politely.

"You went to high school with my cousin. I saw your picture in the yearbook."

He tilted his head. "Who's your cousin?"

"Ray Garrett."

Jack thought for a moment and then smiled. "I remember Ray. We played baseball together."

"Yeah. Ray said that you were a nice guy…and that I could trust you."

"What's your name?"

"Amanda Garrett."

Her eyes were big and brown and full of innocence—yet Jack got the distinct feeling that they had seen things that weren't. "How can I help you?"

She began twisting the strap of her purse, winding it around her fingers.

"It's all right," he said, seeing that her knuckles were turning purple. "Just tell me what's wrong."

She let the strap fall to the table. "Marissa Thomas was my best friend."

Jack slowly sat forward.

"The week before she died she told me that she had seen something bad happen at the marina."

"What did she see?"

Her lips, and hands, began to tremble. "She was so scared."

"Amanda?" he said in a soft voice. "What did she see?"

"I don't know. She wouldn't tell me. But I think it had something to do with that girl's murder."

"Listen," he said, swallowing his anxiousness, "I want you to tell me from the very beginning exactly what Marissa told you."

"Some nights we liked to hang out around the marina. You know, trying to hook up with a guy. Except, this time she went by herself because I had to work. The next morning, she came over and was like, all freaked out."

"When was this?"

She hugged herself tightly. "Three Thursdays ago."

"What exactly did she say to you?"

She began to shake her head. "Just that she had seen something bad at the marina. She wouldn't say what. She said she couldn't tell me."

"And she used the word, marina? Not lake, or dock—"

"Marina," she replied curtly. "I know what she said."

"When was the last time you saw or spoke with her?"

"It was the morning of the ninth. We walked to the gas station around the corner from our street to get some cigarettes. Then I caught the bus to work and she said she was going home…that was the last time I saw her."

Jack scribbled her words on the pad in front of him as quickly as he could.

"Sir?"

He quit writing and looked up.

"I think she saw that girl being murdered…and I think the killer *knew* she saw him. I believe that's why she was so upset."

"Why didn't Marissa tell the police all this?"

"She didn't think anyone would believe her. She'd been arrested before."

"Why didn't you come to us when she first went missing?"

She looked at him solemnly for a moment, the weight of her burden apparent on her face. "I don't know," she answered quietly. "I guess I was too afraid."

"Afraid of the police?"

"No." She shook her head. "Marissa was absolutely terrified of whatever it was she saw. I didn't want nothing to do with it."

~

Jack leaned against the wall in Nathan's office. Amanda had refused to let anyone drive her home, and had left on foot about an hour ago. "Do you think this guy killed Marissa to cover his tracks?"

Nathan scratched the back of his neck and nodded. "If this girl is telling you the truth, then yeah, that's *exactly* what I think."

Jack picked up Missy Rosenberg's file and scanned the notes. "The timeline fits. Amanda said Marissa was upset three Thursdays ago. That would have been June fifth, the day we found Missy Rosenberg's body."

Nathan studied the calendar on his desk. "Jensen said Marissa was killed around the ninth or tenth. That makes it only a few days between their deaths—not the usual eight."

"It means that the killer got scared and panicked."

"What I don't understand," Nathan said, shaking his head, "is why she went back down there. If she was so afraid, why go back? It just doesn't make any sense."

"It's possible she was taken there from her house or neighborhood. The guy may have been following her."

He folded his arms and sat on the edge of his desk. "Why don't you go to the gas station Amanda said they went to, and see if you can verify that they were there that day?"

~

Nathan wound his way through a sea of people as he walked down the ramp towards the marina.

Several young boys on skateboards saw him approaching and swerved to a stop. They picked up their boards and ran for the parking lot.

The marina was home to several businesses. There was *Sam's* which was the main hub. It rented pontoons and Jet Skis and had everything you could possibly need for an outing on the lake. Next door was *The Sea Shack,* a popular restaurant among tourists and locals alike. These two places were the anchors for the marina, having been a staple for several years.

The rest of the boardwalk was littered with small shops selling everything from t-shirts to corn-dogs. Some of these ventures thrived, others did not. When one closed down, however, it wasn't long before another one opened in its place. It was hard to keep track of them all.

The unmistakable roar of speedboats sounded up ahead as he went through the gate that led to the marina. The water around the docks smelled of dead fish and marine fuel. Throw in the ninety-degree heat, and it made for a sickening combination.

As he neared the marina, he saw a boy with blond hair kneeling on the dock.

"Excuse me," he said, flashing his badge. "Can I ask you some questions?"

The boy looked up at him as he tethered a Jet Ski to its cleat. "I guess."

"Do you work here?" Nathan asked, noticing his shirt had *Sam's* written on it.

"Yeah." He stood up, revealing how tall he was. "What's your name?"

"Jeremy Sanders."

Nathan reached inside the folder he had tucked under his arm and pulled out the photo of Marissa Thomas. This time it was her senior picture from the high school yearbook instead of the one from the morgue. "Do you know this girl?"

"Sorry," he said, shaking his head.

Nathan noticed he'd answered before he ever saw her face. "How old are you, Mr. Sanders?"

"Twenty."

"Did you go to high school here?"

"Yeah."

He held the picture up for him again. "So did this girl. Are you sure that you've never seen her?"

The boy swallowed nervously. "I think maybe she was a couple of years behind me."

Nathan stared at him, wondering why he had lied just now. "Did you ever see her hanging around down here?"

"Um...yeah. I used to see her around sometimes."

"What about on June ninth? Do you remember seeing her then?"

A smile spread across his face. "Man, I don't keep track of the days. It's crazy around here in the summer."

"Do you remember the last time you saw her?"

"Hey, Sanders! I need you inside!"

155

Jeremy turned around when he heard Sam Bryant's voice. "I'm sorry, I've gotta get back to work."

Nathan grabbed his arm, stopping him. "Answer my question first."

His smile faded quickly. "I don't remember the last time I saw her."

~

Before Nathan could get back to the station he had to drive out to a remote part of town to serve an arrest warrant for unpaid parking tickets.

He turned off the main highway and onto a dirt road. The lack of rain immediately caused a thick cloud of dust to invade his open window.

As he pulled up to the house, a large black dog came from around the corner and began snarling. The hair on its back stood on end as it bared its teeth to him.

Nathan thought twice about opening his door. Getting bitten by a dog today was not on his agenda. He leaned his head out the window. "Nice dog. Nice doggie."

Upon hearing him speak, the dog stopped snarling and began wagging its tail.

Nathan cautiously opened the door and stepped out. He stood still, allowing the dog to sniff his work boots and jeans. Stealing a quick glance towards the front of the house, it didn't appear as if anyone was home.

The dog followed on his heels as he made his way across the yard. "Mr. Lawler?" He banged on the door. "This is Chief Sommers. I've got a warrant for your arrest."

When there was no answer, he went around to the back and knocked louder. "Mr. Lawler?" He rested his hand on his Glock and turned around. This was a true waste of an afternoon.

As he stepped off the porch, the dog came bounding up with an old tennis ball in his mouth. Nathan couldn't help but smile when he dropped it at his feet. He picked up the slobbery thing and tossed it a few feet into the grass.

With a skittering of his paws, the dog bounded after it.

Nathan's eyes were suddenly drawn to the brilliant blue sky above him. The clouds stretched for what appeared to be miles and miles as they filled the horizon. From where he was standing, it looked as if they were touching the rolling green prairie that lay just beyond Mr. Lawler's backyard.

Seeing this was nearly an everyday occurrence for him, yet there were times that it still took his breath away.

"I told you Montana was gorgeous," Jenny said, *smiling.*

He put his arm around her waist and nodded. "It certainly is."

"They don't call it Big Sky for nothing." She gestured with her hand. "Here comes the best part."

Nathan stood in silent wonder as the sun began to rise. Within a few minutes, it had ascended into the cloud-filled sky highlighting them in a delightfully purplish hue.

She laid her head upon his shoulder. "It's beautiful, isn't it?"

"Yes," he whispered. "But not nearly as beautiful as you are, Mrs. Sommers."

"I like the way you say that."

His thumb felt of the wedding band on his finger. It was still an odd sensation. He pulled her closer to him and kissed her softly.

"Do you realize that we've been married for exactly thirty-six hours and seventeen minutes?"

He laughed. "Has it been that long?"

She turned slightly and looked at the sky once more. "I wish we could always have this."

"What's that?"

"This. The way we feel about one another right now."

He tilted his head and smiled. "It's only going to get better."

"I hope, later on, you don't have any regrets that I talked you into moving here."

"Why would you think that?"

She shrugged. "I know you liked being on the force in Sacramento."

He cupped her face in his hands and stooped to catch her gaze. "Jenny, I would have moved to Antarctica to be with you. I don't regret anything. I'm looking forward to being the chief of police of Silver Creek. And I know how long you've wanted to come back here and teach." He paused and shook his head slightly. "But I don't think your father likes me very much."

"He likes you," she said, giggling. "You'll just never get him to admit it."

"Well, that's reassuring."

Jenny suddenly wrapped her arms around him and hugged him tightly.

He bent down and kissed her on the lips, pressing his body close to hers.

"I will always love you, Nathan," she said, drawing back to look at him. "Till death do us part."

He kissed her on the forehead and smiled back. "Till death do us part."

A bitter sigh fell from him. He remembered how easily those five words had rolled off his tongue at the church, never giving any thought whatsoever to their meaning...until now.

~

Jack sat in the corner chair in the interrogation room rubbing his temples as he watched the security tapes from *The Quickie Mart*. Staring at the monitor for the past two hours had given him a headache.

The smell of hamburgers began to fill the room and he turned to see Nathan coming in carrying a white sack.

"Had any luck?" he asked, sitting down across from him.

"No," Jack answered, reaching into the sack. He quickly unwrapped the burger and bit into it. "I have to go slow and there were a lot of people that visited *The Quickie Mart* on the morning of the ninth."

Nathan took a big bite out of his own hamburger.

"Did you bring in Mr. Lawler?"

He shook his head. "Nobody was home except his dog."

Jack's cell phone rang. A smile formed on his lips when he saw who the caller was. "Hi, sweetheart."

Nathan took another bite, trying not to listen.

"I'm having a burger with Nathan right now. What are you doing? … No, I haven't had a chance to ask him yet." He looked over at him and flashed a grin. "She wants to know if you're going to come over for dinner on Sunday. She promises there won't be any surprises."

Nathan smiled and nodded.

"He's nodding his head yes. Okay. I'll call you when I'm headed home tonight. … Love you too." Jack slipped the phone back in his pocket and laughed. "That woman is all torn up because she thinks you're mad at her."

"She's hard to stay mad at," he said, taking the last bite of his burger. "Besides, I miss her cooking."

Jack leaned back against the chair and stretched. "Are you going to see Katie this weekend?"

He stopped chewing and looked up, startled by the question.

"Girls *talk* to each other, Nathan."

He forced the chunk of meat down his throat and crumpled the wrapper between his fingers.

"Well?" Jack prompted.

His mouth twitched as he stood to go. "I'm thinking about it."

Chapter Seventeen

Katie stood in her bathroom Saturday evening fussing with her hair. She couldn't decide whether to wear it pulled back in a ponytail, or down around her shoulders. After a few more moments of indecisiveness, she decided to wear it down.

Ding-dong!

She hurriedly applied her lipstick and ran to answer the door.

Nathan stood on the other side looking about as nervous as she felt.

"Hi," she said, taking a step back to let him in.

"You look very nice."

"Thank you," she answered, noticing that he was wearing a light blue button-down that matched his eyes perfectly.

After leaning over to greet Lance, he straightened up and smiled. "Are you ready to go?"

~

Katie and Nathan sat in a corner of *The Sea Shack* near the rear entrance. There were a lot of people here this evening, but the waiter had seated them right away.

"That badge must get you a lot of perks."

"Why's that?"

"We didn't have to wait in line."

He shrugged. "I guess it has its advantages."

Katie placed her elbows on the table, letting her eyes wander around the restaurant. It seemed to her that the owner had gone to a great deal of trouble to make the place resemble a real shack. The walls were covered in crooked weather-worn planks and old sea memorabilia. She stared at the large fish mounted on the wall above Nathan's head and determined that it was the most hideous-looking creature she had ever seen.

The one redeeming quality it held was the floor to ceiling windows that covered both sides of the establishment. It gave off a beautiful panoramic view of the crystal blue water. "It's really pretty here, don't you think?"

Nathan glanced out the window and then back at her. "Mmm-hmm." Lately, the only thing the water meant to him was another dead body. He didn't think he could ever view the lake in a good way again.

After the waiter had come and taken their order, Katie noticed several people looking their way. They were trying to be inconspicuous about it but were doing it just the same. Nathan seemed to notice it as well and adjusted the collar of his shirt.

She took a sip of her water, trying to dismiss it. "So, why don't you wear a uniform like your deputies?"

"Because I'm the chief," he said, grinning at her, "I don't have to wear one."

"Is that another perk?"

"Absolutely." He cocked his eyebrow. "But I can get a cowboy hat if you like."

"Now that I'd like to see," she said, laughing.

Nathan leaned back in his chair. "I know that Cheryl told you all about me. But I know next to nothing about *you*, except that you hail from Seattle."

"What would you like to know?"

"Mmm," he said, pursing his lips. "Do you have any brothers or sisters? Or any boyfriends—ex, or current—floating around?"

"No, and no."

"Where did you learn to cook so well? Did you go to a culinary school?"

She tilted her head and smiled. "Are you interrogating me?"

He smiled back at her. "I'm very good at it. Don't you think?"

She giggled. "I lived with my grandparents growing up. My grandmother was the one who taught me how to bake. We used to spend hours in her tiny kitchen mixing up batter for cookies..."

Nathan listened to the sound of her voice as she spoke, nearly drowning in its sweetness.

"...she made everything from scratch. She always said that it tasted better that way because of the work that was put into it. "

"Your grandmother seems like a very wise woman."

"She was." Her eyes grew distant for a moment. "Things were so much simpler when I was seventeen. I just didn't know it at the time."

He nodded in agreement. *"Everything* was simpler when we were younger."

She played with the straw in her glass, sliding it up and down. "Do you like to cook, Nathan?"

"I like to cook Pop-Tarts."

Her nose crinkled up as she began to laugh.

"Excuse me."

She was still laughing when she looked up at the tall stranger standing beside their table.

A distinguished man with graying hair smiled down at them. "How are you doing this evening, Nathan?"

He cleared his throat and nodded. "Just fine, Mayor."

There was a long and awkward silence as Katie waited for Nathan to introduce her, but he made no motion to do so.

The mayor extended his hand. "I don't believe I've had the pleasure of meeting you."

Nathan opened his mouth. "This is —"

"I'm Tom Manning, Mayor of Silver Creek," he said, cutting him off.

"Katie Winstead," she said, taking his hand.

"Katie Winstead," he repeated. "Your name sounds familiar."

Nathan watched him with contempt.

"I just bought the bakery on Main Street."

"Ah, yes! I love your pastries!" he said, patting his waistline.

"Oh, well thank you."

He gave her his best smile. "Well, I'll let the two of you get back to what you were doing." He glanced at Nathan as he turned to go. "Be sure and come by my office Monday morning. We need to go over the plans for the Fourth."

"Will do."

Katie witnessed their exchange. It was anything but friendly.

Nathan watched him walk away, and then lowered his gaze.

She noticed that the people who had been staring earlier were now also whispering, but made no attempt this time to pretend that they weren't.

~

After dinner, the two of them made their way along the boardwalk. The sun was beginning to sink slowly behind the trees, giving off a blinding light as it bounced off the water. Katie squinted, wishing she'd thought to bring her sunglasses.

There hadn't been a whole lot of conversation after the mayor had left. They had made idle chit-chat as they ate, but it seemed to her that it had been forced.

As they neared the end of the pier, Nathan turned to her. "I'll be right back."

She watched him head over to a small gumball machine and deposit a quarter.

He returned with his hands cupped together. "Here you go."

Katie held out her hands as he filled them with little brown pellets. "What's this?"

"It's duck food." He put his arm around her waist and led her to the edge of the dock.

She put one hand over her eyes to shield them from the glaring sun. A few yards away, she saw several ducks milling about.

Nathan threw a few morsels into the lake.

They immediately began swimming towards them, each one jockeying for position.

The first one to arrive was a very large, very obese, white duck. It stuck his long neck out and grabbed the piece of food as it floated in the water. "Quack!"

Katie threw some in front of him and laughed as he dove for it. "That one doesn't miss very many meals, does he?"

Nathan smiled down at her. "No. He's the fattest one of the bunch, but he's also the *fastest*. I think he's got a trolling motor under his tail."

She giggled at the thought.

He tossed the last of what he had into the water and brushed his hands against his jeans. He then looked out across the lake for a long time.

Even though he was standing right next to her, Katie couldn't help feeling that he wasn't there. "Nathan? Is everything all right?"

He shifted his eyes towards her and shook his head. "I'm sorry. I know I haven't been very good company this evening."

"Does it have something to do with the mayor?"

A small sigh escaped his lips. "Tom Manning is...*was* my father-in-law."

"Oh." It was the only word she managed to get out.

"He just caught me off guard tonight. It has nothing to do with you." He took a step closer. "I really enjoyed this evening, and I—"

A loud beeping noise came over his radio. "Chief Sommers? Do you copy?"

Nathan frowned when he heard the central dispatcher's voice. On the weekends, 911 calls were sent there and then dispatched accordingly. "This is Sommers. Go ahead."

"There's a 211 in progress, at the *Pick N Save* on Second and Beaumont."

He looked at Katie, his expression serious. "Can you take a cab home?"

She nodded.

"Are you sure?"

"Go ahead. I'll be fine."

"I'm sorry," he said, bringing the radio to his lips. "10-4. I'm on my way."

"Copy that. Backup is en route."

Katie watched as he turned and began running at full speed down the boardwalk before heading up the ramp.

~

Nathan drove code three as hard as he could towards the *Pick N Save*. There had been a rash of convenience store robberies the last few months in this area.

As he drew closer, he heard Collins come over the radio. "Be advised, suspect is fleeing on foot down the alley behind Beaumont. Officer in pursuit!"

Nathan made a sharp turn and sped down Second Street in hopes of cutting him off. He jumped out of his truck and ran down the back alley behind the store.

He heard shouting around the side of the building, followed by heavy footsteps.

The suspect emerged from around the corner and skidded to a halt when he saw Nathan.

"Police, get down on the ground now!" he yelled, drawing his weapon.

The suspect took a step backward and pivoted around to run.

Jack came upon his blind side, tackling him to the ground.

The man tried to push himself up, but Jack pressed his knee into his spine, using all his weight to hold him still.

Nathan holstered his weapon and knelt beside him to help. It was then that he noticed the blood dripping from his deputy's forehead. "You all right?"

He nodded as he reached for his handcuffs. "He got the drop on me with his gun. He tossed it near the dumpster back that way," he said, trying to catch his breath.

"You got him?"

"Yeah."

Nathan stood up and ran down the other alleyway. The dumpster was overflowing, but that hadn't stopped people from throwing their trash beside it.

He sighed as he began sifting through the boxes and sacks one by one. Looking for a gun in a pile of garbage was not an easy task. To make matters worse, the dumpster was owned by the restaurant next door. The smell of rotting food was overwhelming in this heat.

"Check underneath."

Turning around, he saw Jack walking towards him with the suspect in tow.

Nathan lay flat on the ground and peered under the dumpster. There it was. He pressed his left shoulder up against the metal as he reached for it. He grasped it with his fingertips and got to his feet. "9 mil," he said, showing it to Jack.

"Same weapon used in the other robberies."

"Hey, man. That's not mine."

They both looked at the suspect. He was tall, skinny, and covered in tattoos.

"Sure it isn't," Nathan said as they led him out of the alleyway.

Jack handed a wad of bills to him. "He had this in his pocket."

"That's *my* money," said the suspect.

"Come on." Jack jerked him towards the street.

The clerk from the *Pick N Save* was waiting for them as they came out of the alley. "That's him," she said, nodding.

"Listen," Nathan said, turning to Jack. "I'll run him in and take care of the paperwork. You need to get to the ER. It looks like you need stitches."

"It's not that bad, is it?" He reached inside the cab of his truck for a tissue and pressed it against his forehead.

"*Jack*. Go to the ER."

He lowered his hand and saw that the tissue was soaked in blood. "All right."

"I'll talk to you later," Nathan said as he began walking the suspect towards his truck on Second Street.

~

The DNA extracted from Marissa Thomas's fingernails had finally come back. A special courier had delivered it about an hour ago. The lab confirmed it belonged to a male; however, without a suspect to match it to, they were still back to where they started.

Nathan stuck the report in Marissa's folder and leaned back in his chair. He stared up at the ceiling in his office, letting his eyes follow the silver bands that held the suspended tiles in place.

He had been here most of the day and had responded to three calls, which was actually pretty slow for a Sunday. He didn't mind being here though, as he had grown to like the solitude he found within the confines of his office. For some reason, being alone here was better than being alone at home.

He also wanted to give Jack as much time with Cheryl as possible before the baby came. Not spending time with Jenny when he had the opportunity, was something he deeply regretted.

He felt Jenny slip her fingers around his neck as she kissed him on the side of his face. "The last day of school is Friday. Have you thought about where we're going for vacation?"

He scooted the kitchen chair back and pulled her into his lap. His hand rested upon her stomach, feeling for any movement.

"Well?" she said, smiling down at him.

"I'm not sure that I can get away for an entire week," he said, picking up his phone.

She wrapped her arms around his shoulders and sighed. "You know our days of just us are about to come to a close."

"Mmm-hmm," he said, scrolling through the numbers on his cell.

She grabbed it out of his hands. "And I'd like to spend a week alone with you."

"I need to make a call, Jenny," he said in an irritated tone.

Her smile faded. "Don't you want to spend time with me?"

He tried to swallow his guilt. "Of course I do." He reached up and touched the side of her cheek. "This just isn't the best time. You know how busy the summers are here."

She set his phone down on the table and got up to check on the casserole she was baking.

"Maybe we can go somewhere in September while you're still on maternity leave," he offered. "I promise we'll do something before you have to go back to teaching."

She kept her back to him as she closed the oven door. "I guess that would be okay."

He heard the hurt in her voice as his phone began to vibrate. Seeing who the caller was, he picked it up and walked out of the room.

Nathan clenched his fists and pressed them against his head as feelings of utter shame descended upon him.

The phone on his desk rang.

"Chief Sommers," he said, wiping his eyes.

"Hey! You're not bailing out on me are you?"

He cleared his throat as the memory began to fade. "No, I'm coming," he said, checking his watch. "Time just got away from me. I'm going to pick up Katie and we'll be there in about twenty minutes."

~

Katie cleared the table as Cheryl rinsed the plates and loaded them into the dishwasher. "Are you getting nervous?"

"A little," she replied, "but I'll be glad to be able to paint my toenails again."

Katie laughed as she handed her a glass.

Cheryl peered through the window over the sink. Jack and Nathan were still sitting on the back porch. She shoved the glass in the top rack and turned to her new best friend. "I've been dying to know how your date went last night!"

Katie leaned against the counter and folded her arms. "It went okay."

A look of disappointment came across her face. "Just okay?"

"I don't know," she said, shrugging. "While we were at the restaurant, the mayor stopped by and talked for a bit. It really seemed to change Nathan's mood."

"Did he tell you about their relationship?" Cheryl asked hesitantly, not wanting to upset Nathan again for divulging too much information.

"You mean about him being his father-in-law? Yeah, he told me last night."

"They never really got along to begin with, and things are pretty tense between them right now because of the murders," Cheryl said.

Katie nodded, seeming to accept the explanation.

"Other than that, how did it go?"

"Well, then he had to respond to that robbery." She suddenly shook her head and began to laugh. "I guess as far as first dates go, it wasn't the greatest."

~

"How did Cheryl take to seeing that?" Nathan asked.

Jack tenderly touched the bandage above his left eye. "She was upset. But she took it better than I expected." He held his bottle of beer between his fingers. "How about you? How did your date go?"

"Mmm, not so well." He took a long swallow of his own beer and sighed. "I had to leave her standing there on the boardwalk when I responded to the 211." He shook his head. "I felt so bad just leaving her there. She must hate me."

Jack smiled at his friend. "She came with you tonight, didn't she?"

"Yeah."

"Well, she *must* like you, or she wouldn't be here." He cocked his head sideways. "Although, I have no idea why."

Nathan laughed and shook his head again. "Me neither." He set his beer between his feet and rubbed the back of his neck for a moment. "I'll be late in the morning. I've got a meeting with the mayor."

"What does he want, now?"

"He wants to square things away for the Fourth of July, but I'm sure it will turn into a discussion about the murders before I leave."

"I'm so sick of these *goddamn* murders."

Nathan looked over at him, surprised by his words. His deputy rarely, if ever, cursed. "We're going to get this guy, Jack. It's only a matter of time."

Jack bowed his head, brushing the neck of the bottle along his brow. He'd wanted to be a police officer for as long as he could remember. And he'd always felt that he was good at his job...until recently. Now, he just covered up the dead bodies and asked questions that led to nowhere. He could sense the town's growing dissatisfaction with the police department as the murder rate climbed. He'd never felt more inadequate.

"Hey, Jack?"

He felt his jaw tighten upon hearing Cheryl's voice. "Yeah?"

"We've got dessert."

The two men stood up and walked back into the kitchen.

Cheryl and Katie were standing by the table. A square cake with chocolate icing was in front of them. "Happy Birthday, Nathan!"

He stopped in his tracks. With everything going on, he had honestly forgotten what today was.

"Make a wish!" Cheryl said.

Nathan pretended to make a wish and then bent down to blow out the candles. "Thanks for only putting three on there."

Katie watched as a smile spread across his face. It was a genuine smile, and she knew that at this particular moment he was happy.

Cheryl held the camera up. "Look this way you two."

Nathan put his arm across Jack's shoulder as the camera flashed.

"So, how old are you?" Katie asked.

"Thirty-four."

"That old, huh?" teased Jack, pushing his misery to the side.

Nathan grinned back at him. "Just remember, buddy, you're gonna catch up to me next month."

~

Later that evening, Katie sat with Nathan on her sofa. He had driven her home about thirty minutes ago, yet seemed in no hurry to leave. At the moment, he was wiggling his finger between the cushions for Lance to grab.

Lance's eyes looked like big green marbles as he waited for just the right moment before pouncing.

"Ow!" Nathan said, rubbing his finger. "He's got some sharp teeth."

"Tell me about it." She laughed.

"Thanks for coming with me tonight," he said, returning his attention to her.

"I had a great time. I just wish I'd known it was your birthday, though. I didn't even get a chance to buy you a present."

He shook his head slightly. "I wouldn't have wanted you to."

Katie propped her elbow up on the back of the cushion. "Why not?"

"I don't deserve one."

"Why do you think that?"

He shrugged. "I left you stranded on the boardwalk last night for one thing."

"I already told you that I'm not mad about that, Nathan. I completely understand." She tilted her head, trying to catch his gaze. "Don't be so hard on yourself."

Lance hopped up on her lap and began kneading his paws on her jeans.

Nathan watched him silently.

"What's the other reason?"

"Hmm?"

"You said, 'for one thing'. What's the other reason you think you don't deserve a present?"

He looked away struggling for an answer.

Katie reached over and took his hand. She gently ran her thumb along the cuts on his knuckles.

Her touch sent a shiver down him, making his pulse race.

"How about one night this week I make you dinner?"

He nodded. "I'd like that."

She suddenly leaned over and kissed him.

The smell of lilacs surrounded Nathan as he kissed her back. She began to awaken feelings in him that he had long forgotten. He closed his eyes, feeling the warmth of her mouth against his.

She slipped her arms around his neck, drawing him against her.

He abruptly pulled back and stumbled to his feet.

"What's wrong?"

"I should probably be getting home," he said, casting his eyes anywhere but on her. "I've got an early meeting in the morning."

"Okay," she said after a long pause.

He muttered a quick goodbye before he left.

~

The quiet greeted Nathan as he came through his front door. His face still tingled from where Katie had kissed him. He tossed his keys on the table and sighed. As if he hadn't given her enough reasons already, she must surely hate him by now.

He made his way into the bedroom and opened the closet. Jenny's clothes hung neatly on the right side, her shoes tucked underneath. An empty cardboard box sat on the floor. Nathan stared at it for a long time. Over the past few months, he had made several attempts to pack her things, but couldn't do it. It made him feel like he was betraying her all over again.

Reaching in, he grasped the sleeve of a red shirt near the back. It was one that she was particularly fond of and had worn often—although the last few months of her pregnancy, she hadn't been able to wear it. He pressed it against his mouth and breathed in. Traces of her perfume still remained.

Nathan's footsteps echoed in the hallways of Highland Elementary as he made his way towards one of the fourth-grade classrooms.

This morning his captain had informed him that he was to speak at Career Day, and all the groaning in the world wasn't going to get him out of it.

He stopped at room 115 and peered through the window in the door. His movement caught the eye of the teacher.

She said something to the class and then came over to let him in. "Good morning. I'm Ms. Manning."

"Detective Sommers," he said, finding it hard not to get lost in her eyes. They were the prettiest shade of blue he'd ever seen. She was wearing a red blouse tucked neatly inside a white skirt that complimented her slender waist.

He suddenly noticed that twenty-five little heads were now leaning forward at their desks staring at him.

"Thank you so much for coming to speak with the class today," she said, holding the door open for him. "Come on in, and I'll introduce you."

He came in just enough for her to shut the door.

"Don't be nervous," she whispered. "They love policemen. Just say a few things about what you do and then they'll hit you with tons of questions."

Before he could reply, she turned and walked away. Her long, shapely legs carried her to the front of her desk as her blonde hair bounced softly upon her shoulders. "Class, this is Detective Sommers. He is with the Sacramento Police."

Her voice rang true of a teacher of young kids. It was silky and soft. Soft, as if he could reach out and feel it.

"I want everyone's attention when he is speaking."

The room fell silent as she motioned for him to come and stand next to her.

He couldn't feel his legs but knew he must be walking because he was drawing closer to her. He managed a small smile and wiped his sweaty palms on his jeans. As he turned to face his interrogators, she began making her way towards the back of the classroom.

He cleared his throat. "How many of you know what a detective does?"

Several hands went up in the air.

He pointed to a dark-haired boy near the front.

"A detective tries to find out who committed a crime."

"That's exactly right." He felt himself relax a little bit. As he continued speaking, his eyes would occasionally fall upon the teacher. She seemed to be listening with great interest.

When he was finished explaining what he did, he fielded questions from them. The class asked him everything from, 'Can I shoot your gun?' to 'Have you ever shot anyone?' And before he knew it, the teacher was having the students thank him for coming.

"All right, class. Line up. It's time for lunch."

Chaos quickly ensued as chairs were pushed back and feet ran towards the door.

After they had quieted down, she herded them out. "I know you're probably pressed for time, Detective, but you are more than welcome to eat lunch with us."

Nathan nodded. "I'd like that." He followed her down the hall, completely entranced by her beauty.

She suddenly turned and smiled. "My name's Jenny, by the way."

He smiled faintly as he let go of her sleeve. She'd always kidded him that their first date had been shared with one hundred and twenty-five students over chicken nuggets and fries.

Chapter Eighteen

Monday morning Nathan sat at the conference table with Betty Sturgis. She was head of the Event Planning Committee, and for the past half hour had been giving him a rundown on the Fourth of July plans for Silver Creek.

Betty was a no-nonsense type. He had met her enough times to call her by her first name, yet she never reciprocated. He figured she must have been wearing the bun in the back of her head too tight because she was absolutely devoid of any personality. She had barely greeted him before she began unrolling her charts.

"The mayor will give his speech at five in the afternoon, and then the festivities will begin. He wants the stage set up over here." She pointed at the green square on the paper. "So, to allow for ample parking, we need Second and Main blocked off."

Nathan stifled a yawn. It was the same as last year and the year before.

"The band will start playing immediately after his speech. And the fireworks will start at nine forty-five." She looked over at him. "Do you have any questions, Chief Sommers?"

He feigned interest in the chart. "No, I think it's pretty cut and dry."

"Good morning, Betty."

Nathan saw an immediate change in her disposition when Manning came through the door.

"Good morning, Mayor," she said demurely.

He walked up to the table and slid his hands in his pockets. "How's it looking, Nathan? Are we good to go?"

"Yeah, we're good to go," he replied, standing up.

"Okay, then," he said, smiling. "Thank you so much for coming by, Betty. And as always, you've done an outstanding job."

"Thank you, Mayor."

As she leaned across the table to gather her things, Nathan caught Manning staring at her ass. He looked away, embarrassed for her.

"Oh, and Chief Sommers, here's an extra copy of the event schedule for you." She smiled sweetly at him as she handed him the paper.

Manning rested his hand on her lower back as he escorted her towards the door.

"We're all looking forward to hearing your speech, Mayor," she said, clutching the charts against her chest.

"Well, I guess I better get busy writing it then."

She giggled playfully at him as he showed her out.

Manning watched her walk down the hall for a moment before shutting the door. His smile turned into a scowl by the time it reached Nathan. "What's the latest on the murders?"

"The DNA found under the fifth victim's fingernails is definitely from a male."

"And?"

At this point in time, Nathan was not about to divulge the fact that Marissa Thomas may have witnessed a murder. He did not want it to be leaked to the public. He already suspected that Mac Hodges had a friend somewhere in this office. "That's all we have right now."

Manning stepped away from the door and made his way towards him. "Well, maybe if you cut back a little on your social life, you might be able to get your job done."

And that's what Nathan had been waiting for. He looked at the schedule Betty had given him for a moment, trying to control his temper. "I'm doing my job, Tom."

"Are you?" His tone was arrogant. "It didn't look that way to me. In fact, it didn't look that way to a lot of people. Think about it for a minute, Nathan. Five women have been murdered, and instead of investigating them, you're out on a *date*."

"Why don't you just come out and say what you really mean and quit hiding behind politics?"

Manning clenched his jaw. "This has *nothing* to do with Jenny."

"The *hell* it doesn't!"

His face darkened. "If you want to continue being the chief of police, then I suggest you get your priorities straight."

"Don't threaten me, Tom." Nathan kept his voice low. "It's beneath you."

~

Jack stared intensely at the computer screen, waiting. "There," he said, pointing with his finger.

Nathan leaned over his shoulder to see.

"There's Marissa Thomas and Amanda Garrett walking into *The Quickie Mart*. But look right here. At the same time they enter the store, this car pulls up."

Nathan looked at the screen as Jack continued.

"The girls spend about three minutes inside the store. No one else enters or leaves during that time. Now watch..."

The two girls went out the door and walked to their left. As they did, the car slowly backed out and went the same way.

"Does the store have any outside cameras?"

"No, just this one."

"Run it back again."

They watched the footage several more times. The car's headlights bounced off the store window, encasing the vehicle in light. That, along with the angle of the security camera, made it virtually impossible to see what type of car it was. It appeared to be an SUV, maybe white or silver in color, but it was just a guess on Nathan's part.

~

Katie was seated at one of the tables near the back of the shop going over her sales for June. The morning rush was over and she had promised herself that she would get this done today. She had learned from experience that staying on top of her financials was a key element to being successful.

She totaled up her receipts and was relieved to find out that she had made enough to at least cover the rent for the building. It was far from being in the black, but she felt that she was off to a good start.

The next task at hand was to place orders for supplies. Keeping up with napkins, straws, and Styrofoam cups was proving to be a challenge, not to mention all the dry goods she needed for baking.

She looked up absently when the door opened.

Nathan was walking towards her.

"Hi," she said, summoning a smile.

He looked at all the papers spread out in front of her. "You look busy."

"I'm just going over month-end," she replied, closing her laptop.

"How's it looking?"

"Not too bad, all things considering."

"That's good news."

"Would you like some coffee?"

"No, thank you."

"Are you sure?" She stood up and started towards the counter. "I've just made a fresh pot."

Nathan held up his hand. "No, I'm fine."

She stopped upon hearing the strange tone in his voice. "Is there something wrong?"

"I just need to talk with you for a minute."

Katie slowly sat back down, getting the distinct feeling that she was about to get the brush off.

He placed his hands on the table and sighed. "I'm sorry I left so abruptly last night."

"It's okay."

"*No*, it's not," he said, shaking his head. "And I know that you're too nice of a person to ever tell me so." He searched for something else to say, but couldn't think of the words to explain himself to her.

They sat without speaking for a long time.

"You never gave me an answer about your birthday dinner," she said, trying to ease the tension. "How about if you come over this Thursday? I mean, if you still want to see me, that is."

Nathan ran his fingers through his hair. She had misunderstood what he was trying to tell her. "I would love to see you Thursday."

"Chief, do you copy?"

He stood up and reached for his walkie-talkie. "Go ahead, Norma."

Katie sighed to herself as she watched him walking away. He was definitely an odd duck.

~

Nathan pulled up outside the apartment complex with his lights flashing.

The same timid man as before met him by the door.

"What's the problem?"

"The tenants in 519 were supposed to have vacated the premises this morning, but the woman's locked herself in there. When I asked her to leave, she threatened me with a butcher knife."

"Where's the boyfriend?"

"I haven't seen him in a few days."

"Do you have the key?"

The man handed it to him.

"I'll need you to stay out here," he said as he turned and hurried up the steps to the fifth floor.

"Ms. White?" Nathan banged on the door. "It's the police. I need you to open this door right now."

There was no answer.

He reached for his radio. "Norma, do you copy?"

"Go ahead, Chief."

"I need backup at my location."

"Copy that. Stand by."

Nathan quietly turned the lock with the key and drew his weapon. He opened the door and scanned the room.

Shauna White stood near the hallway by the living room holding a large knife in her hands.

"Get out! I already told that landlord, and now I'm tellin' you. I am not leaving this apartment."

He could hear her little girl crying in one of the bedrooms behind her. "Where's Miguel?"

"He got arrested over in Custer last week. I didn't have the money to get him out on bail."

"Ma'am, I realize how upset you are, but this isn't going to help you or your daughter right now," he said in a gentle voice. "I need for you to put down the knife."

She shook her head. "I'm *not* leaving."

"Is there a relative or friend that the two of you can stay with for a few days?"

"No." Her chin trembled slightly. "We don't have anywhere else to go."

"Chief? Backup is en route."

"10-4." Nathan clipped the radio back on his belt and holstered his Glock, trying not to intimidate her any further. "Is your little girl all right?"

"She's fine. She's just scared."

He began walking towards her, his hands out to his sides. "Shauna, you need to put down the knife."

"Stay back!" She clutched the long wooden handle, wielding it in front of her like a sword.

He stopped when he got within reach.

"We just need a few more days to make the rent. I told that stupid landlord, but he wouldn't even listen!" Her hands began to shake as she waved the knife at him. "Can you talk to him for me?"

The sirens could be heard in the distance.

"I'll see if I can get him to change his mind." Nathan suddenly looked past her shoulder and nodded. "Right now, your little girl needs you."

The woman instinctively looked behind her.

Nathan lunged forward and grabbed her forearm with both hands. In one swift motion, he lowered her arm and slammed it hard against his upcoming knee.

She cried out in pain as the knife clattered to the floor.

He pinned her against the wall as he kicked the weapon away with his boot.

Her body suddenly became wracked with sobs as he turned her around to place the handcuffs on her.

"Chief?"

He glanced over his shoulder. "Check the bedrooms, Collins."

Jack hurried past him and down the hallway. A moment later he came back carrying the girl. "She's okay."

"What are you doing with my baby?" Shauna screamed.

The toddler began to wail as she stretched her tiny hands out for her mother to take her.

Jack held her tightly against him as she struggled to get out of his arms.

"You put her down right now you *son-of-a-bitch!*" She lunged forward, but Nathan held her as Jack walked out of the apartment.

"You *can't* take her! Please don't take my baby!" she sobbed. "Please don't take her!"

A crowd of people had gathered by the time they got to the parking lot.

She turned towards him as he opened the door of his truck. "Please don't take her from me," she begged.

Nathan's heart broke for her. She had gotten herself in a bad situation that was about to get worse. Putting her in jail meant social services would take her daughter. This was sometimes a necessary action, but it wasn't always what was best. He put her in the backseat and pulled out his cell phone.

Jack held the little girl against his chest as he sat behind the wheel in his own truck. He could smell her urine-soaked diaper. "It's okay," he said softly, patting her on the back. "It's all right."

She suddenly put her hands against him and pushed herself up. Her face was red and splotchy as her eyes brimmed with tears. "Momma."

He kissed her gently on her cheek and nodded. "I know. You want your mommy."

Nathan slipped his phone back into his pocket and walked over to speak with the landlord.

"Is she going to jail?"

"That all depends on you, and whether you're going to press charges."

The man looked past him and into the window of the truck. His hands fretted together. "No. I won't press charges as long as she understands she can't come back here."

~

A few minutes later, Nathan led Shauna White up the rickety porch steps of a rundown two-story home. She hadn't said a word to him since he had put her in the truck.

The screen door creaked open and a short woman with a shock of fiery red hair stepped outside to greet them. "Chief Sommers."

"Hello, Miss Hattie. This is Shauna White, the one I called you about."

Jack pulled up behind Nathan and carried the little girl across the front yard.

"Well, let's not stand around in this godforsaken heat," Hattie said, opening the door for them.

The girl started crying again when she saw her mother standing next to Nathan. "Mommy!"

"She's coming," Jack said, following Hattie inside.

Nathan took her handcuffs off and turned her so she could see him. "Ms. White, you can stay at this shelter for as long as you need to. They can help you get back on your feet."

She started up the steps but stopped and turned around. "You think you're doing me a *favor?*"

Before he could answer, he felt the sting of her hand as it fell hard across his face.

"You think you're my savior? *Huh?* Is that it? You think you're being a hero?"

He looked back at her, not knowing what to say.

She spat on his shirt. "Well, I don't need no savior, and I sure as hell don't need no *fucking hero!*"

~

Nathan's day didn't get any better. That evening, he was headed for home after depositing Mr. Lawler in jail for the unpaid parking tickets. Fortunately, Lawler had gone peacefully, but not before giving him a long speech laced with colorful profanity.

He was deep in thought as he drove along, not really paying attention to the road. His mind went from the murders to Shauna White to Katie—and then started all over again.

A stop sign suddenly caught his eye and he stomped on the brake. His truck came to a screeching halt just before the beginning of the intersection.

Nathan checked his rearview mirror and was relieved to see that no one was behind him. He looked past the stop sign and saw that Blossom Lane was just on the other side. He pressed his foot on the accelerator.

Modest, but well-kept homes lined this quiet neighborhood as he drove slowly through it. Small pink-and-white petals littered the sidewalks from the trees that had been strategically planted on both sides of the street. Their long, slender branches extended out like delicate fingers that nearly touched one another.

He pulled over against the side of the curb and got out. A cool wind hit him as the skies began to turn dark.

As he walked along the lane, he came to a slight bump in the pavement where the new road met the old. Nathan stopped and ran the bottom of his boot across it.

A few years ago, the city had determined that an access was needed for the interstate. It had gotten the entire neighborhood in an uproar, and despite months of protests, the city council went ahead with their plans. Junction 143 was created all in the name of tourism.

A large oak tree stood in a small patch of grass where the new road took a sharp turn. Its trunk was at least four feet in diameter and was estimated to be over two hundred years old. A group of environmentalists had rallied for weeks to save the tree from demolition, and after much deliberation, the city council agreed to let it remain. The tree, which used to grace the end of the lane, now stood by itself on the other side of the junction.

He looked down at the pavement in front of it. The skid marks had long faded away, but the curb held a deep, jagged crack in it.

Why Jenny had come this way that night was a question he would never know the answer to. He stood in front of the tree for a long time. Part of its bark had been stripped away where the front of the car had impacted it. He reached out and felt of the bare wood with his hand, letting his fingers softly touch upon the dark circle. It bore the same scars over its heart that Nathan had on his. The tree was slowly dying.

There were times that he felt the world would be better off if *he* were dead. It seemed to him that it would be penance for his sins.

A drop of water trickled down his face. He held his breath, trying to suppress the sob that would inevitably follow. All the things that he should have told her, but never said. All the things that he should have done, but never did. His hands pressed against the wood as he bowed his head. "I'm so sorry, Jenny." His tears fell one by one onto the ground. "I'm so sorry."

Chapter Nineteen

It was late Wednesday as Katie finished wiping down the counter in the back of the bakery. The rain made a shushing noise as it fell steadily upon the asphalt roof. She hadn't intended to be here this long, but a last-minute order for four-dozen of her double chocolate chip cookies was something she couldn't refuse. They needed to be ready first thing in the morning.

She peeked inside the large commercial oven mounted on the wall. They were looking, and smelling, good, and only needed about two more minutes.

The bell on the front door jingled softly, reminding her that she should have closed up fifteen minutes ago. She wiped her hands on her apron and hurried towards the doorway, but before she could get out front, she heard the bell ring again.

She stepped behind the counter and looked around. The shop was empty and quiet. Whoever it was must have realized that she was closed and left. She went up to the door and turned the lock before flipping the sign over on the window.

She then walked briskly back to the kitchen to get the cookies out of the oven. As she was reaching in for the first tray, the bell on the door rang quietly. She set the pan down on the steel counter and spun around.

With trembling legs, she peered out into the storefront, her eyes searching. No one was in here. Fear gripped her as she hurried towards the front door only to find it unlocked. She turned it once more and ran back to the kitchen. Her hands jerked open the oven and pulled out the remaining trays of cookies. Nearly all of them were burnt around the edges as she slid the pans onto the counter one by one.

She turned off the oven and glanced around. The kitchen had a back door, but if she went out that way, she would have to walk through a darkened alley to get to her car. Deciding against it, she grabbed the keys from her purse and hesitantly stepped once more through the doorway to the front.

She looked down the wall at the end of the counter. The restrooms were on the right-hand side. Maybe whoever it was had come in just to use the bathroom.

Katie's breath quivered as she approached the front door. She was too afraid to go outside, but even more afraid to stay in here. Her eyes searched across the street, hoping to see Nathan's light on in his office window, but the station house was dark. Swallowing her panic, she turned her attention towards her car, which was parked about fifteen feet away.

Steeling herself, she quickly exited and turned to lock the door. It was a difficult thing to do because the key was slightly bent and always took several jiggles and twists to get the latch to turn. It was something that she had been meaning to get fixed but hadn't gotten around to doing.

Her hands shook as she tried to get it to turn. She glanced up and down the street. The heavy clouds had covered the moon making it difficult to see anything. As she turned back around to concentrate on the lock, the unmistakable smell of cigarette smoke surrounded her. A single street lamp captured a long shadow around the corner of the building. Her heart leaped into her throat as the silhouette of a person became apparent.

Katie desperately began wiggling the key trying to force the lock. Finally, she heard it click. She looked to her left as she turned away from the door. The figure was still there.

Her cell phone suddenly rang out nearly causing her to drop her keys. Her fingers dug into the side pocket of her purse. "Hello?" she said as loudly as she could.

"Hey, it's Cheryl."

Katie held her breath as she ran towards her car. Fear forced her to look over her shoulder as she jerked the door open. The shadow was gone. She could hear heavy footsteps retreating in the other direction. Clambering into her car, she slammed the door and pushed the lock button down.

"Katie?"

She jammed the key into the ignition and started the car. "I'm here" — her voice shook — "just heading home from the shop."

~

Fifteen minutes later, Nathan sat at Katie's kitchen table listening to her tell him what had happened. He tried to keep his face emotionless but was having a difficult time. The realization of what could have happened to her hit him hard.

He stood up and pulled his cell phone from his pocket. "Hoskins? I need you to do me a favor."

Katie clasped her fingers together to try and keep from shaking as Nathan asked his deputy to go to the bakery and check things out. Unable to sit still, she got to her feet and hugged herself tightly. She couldn't think of a time when she had been so scared.

She suddenly felt his arms around her shoulders. They were strong and comforting.

"It's okay now," he whispered.

Katie felt his breath, warm and gentle, falling around her as he held her in his arms. "Thank you for being here, Nathan." She gave him a trembling smile as she turned to face him.

"There's no place else I'd rather be."

His eyes were transfixed on her in such a way that she thought he was going to kiss her. After a few seconds of awkwardness, however, she realized that wasn't the case. "Well," she said, taking a step back. "I've got some baking to do."

"Is there anything I can do to help?" he asked. "I mean, besides stay out of your way?"

She reached into the cabinet above her. "Can you get out the eggs and margarine for me?"

"I can do that," he said, heading towards the fridge.

Katie measured and poured a cup of brown sugar in a large mixing bowl as he set the items on the counter for her. "I'll need a half cup of margarine," she said, opening up the carton of eggs.

Nathan held up the stick of butter as he studied the markings on the wrapper. "How do you get a half-cup out of this?"

She glanced sideways at him. "A half-cup is exactly one stick."

"Oh. Well, here you go then."

She unwrapped it, and let it fall into the bowl. "Can you stir this together for me?" she asked, handing him a large spoon.

He looked over at her and smiled. "I can do that."

After they'd mixed together the rest of the ingredients, Katie put a bit of the dough into the palm of her hand. "Now you take the dough and roll it into a ball...like this," she said, demonstrating how.

"Got it."

She spooned some dough into his open hand and watched as he began to form it.

Nathan heard her giggling. "What?"

"You're making it look like a snake. It's supposed to be a ball."

He looked down at the dough. It did look like a snake — with brown spots.

"Here," she said, cupping her hands over his. She began moving his palms in a circular motion, pressing downwards.

Her touch sent shockwaves through him, electrifying his senses.

"There," she said, opening his hands. "A perfect ball." When he didn't say anything, she glanced up and saw that he was staring at her.

He placed the ball of dough on the cookie sheet and bent down to kiss her.

She closed her eyes as his lips lightly grazed hers. It lasted for only a moment, and then he pulled back.

"You're very beautiful," he said softly.

She felt her cheeks turning red as she fumbled for something to say. Before she could respond, he began to form another ball in his hands.

He looked over at her and smiled. "I think we should make a few snakes."

They got the first two-dozen cookies in the oven and set about mixing up another batch. As they worked together, Katie noticed Nathan's yawns were becoming more prevalent.

"Why don't you go on in the living room? I'm almost done here."

"I don't want to abandon you in your time of need."

"I just have one more tray to go, and then I'll be done."

"You talked me into it," he said, wiping his hands on a towel. "Come on, Lance. Let's go sit down."

Lance's ears perked up at the sound of his name.

Katie laughed as he followed Nathan into the living room like a puppy.

He sat down on the sofa and took off his boots. Spying the remote, he began flipping through the channels until he found ESPN.

Lance jumped up beside him and plopped himself down in his lap.

Nathan listened to Katie rattling around in the kitchen as the sports announcer relayed the latest scores…

It was nearly midnight when Katie took the last batch out of the oven. Forty-eight perfectly baked cookies lay on the counter in front of her, along with four snake cookies.

She looked around her kitchen and sighed. Emotionally and physically drained, she promised herself that she would clean up the mess in the morning.

When she walked out of the kitchen, she saw that Nathan was stretched out on her sofa sound asleep. Lance lay curled up in a ball on his chest. Unable to bring herself to wake him, she covered him with a blanket and turned off the television.

Chapter Twenty

Nathan woke up the next morning to the smell of bacon and eggs. He felt a smile forming. He liked the summers, as Jenny always had time to have breakfast with him. He opened his eyes and sat up, searching the room for her.

"Good morning."

His face betrayed him as he tried to keep his smile.

Katie bent down and swept his brown locks from his forehead. "Are you all right?"

"What time is it?" he asked, searching for a clock.

She set the plate on the coffee table. "It's still early. I'm sorry, but I have to get the cookies over to the bakery."

He slipped on his boots, trying his best not to look at her.

She sat down next to him, positioning her body close to his.

"Thanks for making me breakfast," he said, bending over to tie the laces.

"Oh, please. It was the least I could do after last night."

Before he could say anything else, she put her arm across his neck and leaned over. Nathan felt his jaw growing rigid as she pressed her lips against his cheek.

"What's wrong?" she asked, drawing back.

"We should probably get going."

"We've got a little bit of time. You can at least have your breakfast," she said, gesturing at the plate.

"Katie...I..." He stopped, not knowing how to begin.

She slipped her hand around his and squeezed. "What's the matter?"

"I need to go." He stood up and walked to the door.

"Will I still see you tonight for dinner?"

He opened the door and bowed his head. "No."

After a long silence, Katie rose from the sofa and made her way over.

Nathan stepped onto the porch and forced himself to look at her. "Will you promise me that you'll get the lock fixed today?"

The bottom of her chin quivered as she closed the door.

~

"Boss!" Hoskins rushed into the station house and skidded to a halt, nearly out of breath.

Nathan set the coffee pot back on the burner and turned around.

"We've got something." He held up a small plastic bag containing what appeared to be a cell phone. "Two boys found it this morning at Graves Landing."

Nathan took the bag and turned it over in his hands. The phone was covered in grass and mud. "Where exactly?"

"It was within a hundred feet from where Carol Fuqua's body was found." Hoskins gestured at the bag. "Last night's rain must have uncovered it."

"See if you can find a charger for it," Nathan said, walking towards the interrogation room.

Hoskins took off in the other direction. "I think I've got one in the truck."

Nathan slipped on a pair of latex gloves and opened the bag. He immediately noticed that the casing on the back of the phone was cracked.

A few minutes later, Hoskins came hurrying in with the charger. "Here you go, Boss."

He snapped the small cord in one end of the phone as Hoskins plugged the other end into the wall socket.

The battery icon immediately began to flash.

Nathan flipped it open and went to the voice mail settings.

A woman's voice came through the speaker. "Hi, this is Carol. Leave me a message."

Hoskins nodded excitedly. "It's her."

Nathan accessed her messages and held his breath.

This time a man's voice came through. "Hey, it's me. Just wondering where you are. Give me a call when you get this."

Seeing that was the only new message she had, Nathan began checking her log as Si sat down beside him.

"Any outgoing calls?"

"It looks like she made several to the same number almost every night, right up until the day she was killed." He pressed another button and looked at the screen. "That number is also on her incoming calls — including the day she died."

"Let's find out who it belongs to."

Nathan reached for the phone on the wall behind him and dialed the number. He waited patiently, but after the tenth ring, it became clear that there would be no answer or voice mail.

"It's probably a disposable," Hoskins said.

"Probably." He hung up and went to check her photos. He pressed the button with his thumb but got an error. He tried it several more times to no avail. Turning the phone on its end, he saw that it was caked in mud where the memory card was stored. He held it upside down and tried to eject it.

A small stream of dirty water spilled out onto the table.

Nathan suddenly stood up and kicked his chair backward. *Everything* led to a dead end.

Hoskins lifted the card from the phone. "Maybe it will work after it dries out," he said quietly.

Nathan nodded, embarrassed. He didn't like losing his temper in front of his deputies.

"Do you want me to have her phone dusted for prints?"

He cleared his throat. "Who do we have available?"

"I can get Forester from McCone over here this afternoon, maybe."

"Yeah, go ahead. I'll have Norma get hold of the phone company. Hopefully, they can track the owner of the other phone."

Hoskins left the interrogation room to go make the call.

Nathan clenched his fists as his emotions raged inside of him like a tempest. He stripped off his gloves and slammed them into the trashcan by his feet.

"Hey, Chief."

He looked over and saw Jack standing on the other side of the table.

"I heard about the phone. This could be the break we've been looking for."

Nathan nodded and sat down.

"What's wrong?"

He rubbed his eyes for a minute and then told his deputy what had happened to Katie last night.

Jack sat in silence for a long time. "Do you think it was our killer?"

"I don't know," he said, shaking his head.

"Chief?" called Norma from the doorway. "You have a visitor."

He looked up to find Katie.

Her eyes went from him to Jack. "I was hoping we could talk for a minute."

Jack pushed his chair back and got to his feet. "How are you this morning, Katie?"

A weak smile formed upon her lips. "I'm fine, thanks. How are you?"

"I'm good," he answered, slipping past her.

Katie came in the rest of the way and closed the door. She folded her arms against her, trying to collect her thoughts.

Nathan stood rigidly by the table.

Deciding that a direct approach would be best, she dug her fingernails into her skin and drew a deep breath. "I like you, Nathan."

He shook his head. "I like you too, Katie. But it's not that simple for me to move forward."

"I know that. I know that this is all very hard for you. I can't imagine what it must have been like to lose your wife and baby..."

He turned away from her.

"But I know that you loved them..." she said, fumbling for the words, "and that you're still hurting." She drew closer to him and placed her hand on his back. "What was her name going to be?"

"It doesn't matter anymore," he said, staring at the wall.

"It matters to me."

He turned to face her. "Please don't be sad for me," he said angrily.

"It hurts me to see you this way," she whispered.

He turned back around and placed his hands on his waist. "I'm *fine*. I've been living with it for a long time now."

She walked around the chair and stood in front of him, forcing him to look at her. "But you're *not* living, Nathan. You're just going through the motions in life. It's not the same." She reached out and touched the side of his face. "I don't know where our relationship is headed. But I can tell you that I've never felt this way about *anyone* before."

He began to shake his head. "There are things about me that you don't know, Katie…"

"Like what?"

He closed his eyes, ashamed.

"You can tell me. It's all right."

He closed his fingers around her wrist and pulled her hand away from his cheek. "I can't do this. I'm sorry."

Katie's vision began to cloud as she slipped out of his grasp.

"I'm sorry," he repeated. "I never meant to hurt you."

She bit down on her bottom lip, absolutely determined not to cry in front of him.

Nathan clenched his jaw as she brushed past him and ran out the door. Turning sideways, he kicked the chair beside him again, sending it skittering across the floor.

~

Cheryl pulled into an empty parking space next to the bakery and eased her way out from behind the steering wheel.

A man with a tool belt wrapped around his waist was kneeling in front of the door. When he saw her approaching, he stood up and held it open for her. "Ma'am."

"Thank you." Walking inside, she could see Katie standing behind the counter attending to a family with three little kids.

Cheryl gave her a wave and plopped herself down in the nearest chair. Her mouth immediately began to water as the smell of brownies — and all things chocolate — filled her senses.

"Thank you," Katie said, handing the man his change. As he collected the treats, she couldn't help noticing that one of his boys was running the entire length of the counter with his nose pressed against the glass.

"Jacob! If you want your brownie, you better get over here."

The boy stopped and ran over to his mother, who was getting the other two children situated at a table in the corner.

Katie cast a disparaging look at the long smear mark that now graced the glass. She then turned towards Cheryl, forcing a smile that she did not feel. "How are you?"

"Tired," she said with a laugh. "What's with your door?"

Katie glanced at the man kneeling outside. "I'm having trouble with the lock sticking," she answered, not interested in retelling what had happened last night. "Can I get you a brownie, or slice of cheesecake?"

"Oh, don't tempt me," she replied, rubbing her stomach. "I just came by to see if you wanted to ride with me to the shower on Saturday."

Katie gave her a blank stare as she sat down across from her. With everything that had happened, she had completely forgotten about her baby shower.

"Anne's house is a little off the beaten path, so I thought we could ride together."

"That would be great, thanks."

"You're welcome," Cheryl said with a nod.

When she made no motion to leave, Katie felt herself cringe, for she knew without a doubt, that within the next five seconds, the conversation was inevitably going to turn to Nathan. These past few days, she had become painfully aware that he was their only link of friendship. "Are you sure I can't get you a brownie?" she asked, wanting to stop it before it got started.

"I'm sure," Cheryl said, giving her an odd look.

Katie's desire to walk away was only outweighed by her need to know the answer to something that she couldn't ask Nathan. She gave a sideways glance at the family to her left, and then lowered her voice. "What was Jenny like?"

A startled expression came across Cheryl's face.

"Never mind," she said, immediately regretting her question. "It's not important."

"No, it's all right," replied Cheryl, tucking a strand of blonde hair behind her ear. "You just caught me by surprise. Why do you want to know?"

By this time, Katie was trying very hard to keep her emotions in check and felt that if she opened her mouth to answer—more than *words* would come rolling out of it.

Cheryl looked at her for a long time, wondering what had brought this on. "Jenny was a very warm and loving person," she began. "Kindhearted and sincere..." A wry smile spread across her lips. "And she had a wicked sense of humor. She always had me in stitches."

Katie nodded, trying to suppress the tears that were forming.

Cheryl's smile faded as quickly as it had come when she realized what she had done. "I'm sorry, Katie."

The bell over the door chimed as the man stepped inside. "All finished, ma'am."

Katie stood up and placed her hand on Cheryl's shoulder. "Thanks for being honest with me."

~

Jack sat down in his chair and sighed. It had been a long and brutal day, and the only thing he wanted was to get through the next five minutes without having to go out on another call.

He took a small sip of his coffee and glanced towards the interrogation room. Bill Forester, the forensics guy from McCone County, was in there dusting Carol Fuqua's phone for prints. Although he appreciated him coming down on such short notice, he sincerely doubted that he was going to find any prints — other than the victim's.

His eyes wandered over to Nathan's office. He was sitting at his desk, staring at the files in front of him. His mood today had been dark, to say the least, but feeling like it had more to do with Katie, than the murders, he'd left him alone.

He got to his feet and hesitantly walked across the floor. He gave a quick knock on the side of the door to get his attention. "Hey, Chief."

Nathan gave him a weary look. "Jack."

"I'm headed home for the night unless you need me to do anything."

"No. I'm waiting for Bill to finish, and then I'm heading home as well."

Jack shifted his feet as he pressed his shoulder against the doorjamb. "Everything okay?"

Nathan leaned back in his chair and rested his hand on his chin. He knew Jack had seen Katie leaving the interrogation room in tears this morning. "Yeah. I'm good," he said after a moment.

Jack pushed himself away from the doorjamb. "Okay, then. I'll see you in the morning."

Nathan nodded. "Have a good night."

~

Nathan wiped a bead of sweat from his lip as he stood waiting on the front step of the women's shelter. As suspected, no foreign prints had been recovered from Carol Fuqua's phone. He reached over and impatiently rang the bell again, feeling as if the day had been nothing but a complete waste.

Eventually, a young woman came to the door.

He pulled his badge off his belt and held it up to her. "I'm Chief Sommers. I'm here to see Miss Hattie."

She gave him a wary look and then took a step back. "She's in the kitchen."

"Thanks."

The woman turned on her heel and ran up the stairs, disappearing from his sight.

As he made his way down the narrow hall, a delicious smell encircled him. He stopped just outside the doorway of the kitchen and peered inside.

Several women were talking softly amongst themselves as they set the table for dinner.

Nathan glanced around the room, taking a moment to study their faces. Unfortunately, he knew a couple of them but didn't see Shauna.

A burst of static came over his radio.

The women suddenly stopped what they were doing and looked over at him.

Nathan's cheeks began to burn as he reached behind him to turn it down. "I'm looking for Miss Hattie."

He felt a hand on the back of his shoulder and pivoted around.

"Chief Sommers. To what do I owe this pleasure?"

Nathan smiled awkwardly at her, and then glanced into the kitchen. The women were still staring.

Hattie took him by his arm and led him down the hallway. "Don't pay them no mind. They're just leery of men right now."

"Is the girl I brought over last night still here?"

"Yeah, she's still here. She's not sayin' much, though."

Relief flooded him to know that she hadn't left.

"They're all angry and scared when they first get here. It just takes time," she explained.

Nathan nodded as he reached for the small sack that he had tucked under his arm. He held it between his fingers for a long time.

"You okay, Chief Sommers?"

"Would you please see that her little girl gets this?" he asked, handing the sack to her.

"I will, but she's right up the stairs," she said, pointing. "You can give it to her yourself if you like."

Nathan shook his head. "I don't think her mother cares to see me right now," he replied, pulling out his billfold. He handed her four twenties and a ten. "I'm sure she needs a few necessities while she's waiting on her things to arrive from her apartment."

Hattie suddenly grinned at him, revealing several holes where her teeth used to be. "I'll see that she gets it."

"Thanks."

After he had gone, Hattie reached into the sack and pulled out a stuffed pink elephant.

~

Jack guided the trimmer along the bottom of his fence in his backyard. Having mowed the grass tonight in record time, he hurriedly began cutting the weeds along the backside of the shed. He still needed to blow off the driveway and water the plants before heading inside to finish putting the crib together.

As he carried the trimmer around to the front of the shed, he saw Cheryl sitting on the porch swing. "How long have you been out here?" he called, walking across the yard.

She scooted over for him. "A couple of minutes."

He fell back against the swing and sighed. "It's hot out here," he said, wiping his sweat away with the bottom of his t-shirt.

She picked a stray blade of grass from off the side of his face, and then gently touched the stitches on his forehead. "Does it still hurt?"

Jack reached for her hand and brought it to his lips. "No."

She looked away.

He heard her take in her breath, but she didn't say anything. And then he heard the unmistakable sound of a sniff. He let go of her hand and put his arm around her. "What's wrong?"

"I miss Jenny," she blurted.

Jack tasted the salt from her tears as he kissed the side of her face. "I know you do, sweetheart." He rested his elbow on the back of the swing and stroked her hair as they slowly rocked back and forth. "What made you think of her?"

"I saw Katie this afternoon, and she was asking me what Jenny was like." Cheryl wiped at her eyes before continuing. "She seemed really upset. Did Nathan say anything to you today?"

"No," he replied in the most casual tone he could find.

"All this time, I thought that I was helping Nathan by setting him up with her." She stopped and shook her head. "But now I realize that I was just being selfish."

"Why would you say that?"

A new batch of tears began spilling down her face. "I miss her, Jack. I miss the four of us being together. I guess I thought that if I could get Nathan to date Katie, things would be the same again." She laid her head against his chest. "I feel like I've hurt them both."

"Sweetheart, that's not true. I know for a fact that Nathan really likes her. He's just having a hard time letting Jenny go."

"I know that he is," she said, sniffling into his shirt. "That's why I should have just left it alone."

Jack brushed away her tears with the back of his knuckle. "You didn't do anything wrong, Cheryl. You had her over for dinner one night. That was all. You didn't *force* them to date. It was their *choice*." He put his hand under her chin and lifted it up so he could see her face. "If they move forward, then that's great. But if they don't, it's not your fault, okay? Please don't cry."

She drew a deep breath and sat back, trying to stop her tears.

"What would you like for dinner?" he asked, hoping to take her mind off it.

"I don't know. I haven't had time to get to the grocery."

"Well, how about if I order Chinese? Hmm?" he asked, arching his eyebrow. "Would the baby like that?"

Before she could answer, he placed his hand on her stomach and bent down.

"Lydia?" he said, speaking into her bellybutton. "Would you like Chinese? Just do one kick for yes, and two kicks for no."

Cheryl began to laugh in spite of herself.

~

Katie lay curled up on her bed as the tears ran down her face and neck. Lance lay next to her providing some much-needed comfort, purring contentedly as she stroked him on his back.

In her lifetime, she had only dated a handful of men, most of whom had been too immature to establish a real relationship with. There were a few, however, that had done a good job of letting her think that they cared. And after they had taken everything they could from her, both emotionally and physically, they stopped coming around.

Her grandmother had told her once that she was far too trusting for her own good. Katie agreed with her but didn't know how to act any other way. It was an unfortunate trait that had evolved over her need to feel loved.

When she was a little girl, her mother had left her on her grandmother's doorstep, promising that she would come back for her. Katie never saw her again.

That was a life-changing moment for a five-year-old, and one that had left an emptiness deep inside of her. It was a void that she desperately wanted filled. She'd fallen hard for Nathan and kept telling herself that he wasn't like those other men. When she'd spoken to him this morning, she had put it all out there on the line for him, leaving her heart exposed and vulnerable. His response had left her hurt beyond words.

She turned over on her side and buried her face in the pillow.

~

Nathan walked silently along the hiking trail near Graves Landing. It was hard to go home when he only had himself for company. His boots crunched softly on the dried leaves as he made his way down the path.

Everything had felt so right when he'd kissed Katie last night, yet Jenny was first on his mind when he woke up this morning. The last thing in the world he wanted to do was hurt Katie, but this had forced him to realize that he wasn't ready to move on.

The mosquitoes came out in droves as the sun began to set. He waved them away with his hand as he came to the end of the trail. The cabins were just a few yards ahead. Most of them appeared empty, which was unusual for this time of year. But then again, in years past, there hadn't been a serial killer on the loose.

A loud squeal caught his attention making him look up. A little girl with pigtails was running in the grass outside one of the cabins.

Nathan started to go to her but stopped when he saw her face. She was grinning from ear to ear. A moment later, a man came running around the side. He scooped her up in his arms and began smothering her with kisses.

This sent the girl into hysterics as she squirmed and giggled.

Unable to stop himself from watching, Nathan stood in the shadows of the trees.

A woman with light brown hair came out the front door. She wrapped her arms around both of them and laughed.

The man bent down and said something to her before kissing her on the lips.

Nathan turned and began walking away. He'd only gone a few yards when he was suddenly overcome with emotion. He stopped in his tracks as feelings of what should have been...turned into what could still be.

Everything was in front of him, laid out like a present. This was his second chance. His feet began to run back down the trail as his heart soared.

~

Katie roused herself off the bed and went to answer the door. She took her fingers and wiped the bottoms of her eyelids before opening it.

Nathan stood before her. His eyes were brightly lit, his breath shallow. He stepped inside and cupped her face in his hands. "Her name was going to be Hannah Elizabeth."

She looked up at him, feeling the sting of tears returning.

He brushed them away with his thumbs. "The feelings I have for you right now scare me," he said in a quivering voice, "but I can't stand being numb anymore, and I can't stand being apart from you." He held her face gently in his hands as he bent down to kiss her.

Katie threw her arms around his neck as he embraced her. She clutched the back of his head as he untucked her shirt and slid his hands around her waist.

Not wanting to give the neighbors a show, she kicked the door shut with her foot before slipping her hands underneath his t-shirt and pulling it over his head.

Nathan leaned against the door and closed his eyes as her tongue grazed over his bare chest. Her breath was warm and soft as she pressed into him.

Feeling the blood rushing to his extremities, he pushed himself away from the door and scooped her up in his arms. His lips locked with hers as he carried her into the bedroom.

Katie waited with anticipation as he slowly unbuttoned her blouse and parted it with his fingers. She flinched as she felt the back of his hand brush against her breasts.

He followed the curve of her body with his finger, stopping at her waistband. With a slight tug, the button gave way and he slid her jeans down. He quickly unsnapped his holster and set it on the nightstand. As he reached for his radio, he felt her hands on his belt buckle.

Their eyes met as she slid his zipper down.

Nathan hooked his fingers inside her panties and pulled them from her hips.

She arched her back as his tongue roamed along her navel, making her want him more than ever.

He parted her legs with his knee as he pressed his weight against her. She drew in her breath as he pushed inside. He took her arms and pinned them over her head, his fingers interlacing with hers.

She began moving her body in rhythm with his as he rocked her back and forth. Her body began to shudder as the feeling started to sweep over her. She closed her eyes and moaned softly as Nathan's breath fell down around her.

Chapter Twenty-one

Jack finished his coffee and reluctantly pushed his chair back.

"What time do you think you'll be home tonight?" Cheryl asked, rinsing her mug out in the sink.

He walked up behind her. "I don't know," he answered, wrapping his arms around her waist. "Probably around ten I guess."

She leaned against him and smiled.

"What are you going to do on your day off?" he asked, kissing the side of her neck.

"Well, I'll probably waddle over to the grocery and dry cleaners, and then come home and clean the house."

"Don't overdo it," he said, cautioning her.

She turned around and pressed her lips to his. "No worries."

"I'll see you later," he said, patting her stomach before heading towards the door.

"You know, I was thinking that we could grill out this Sunday."

He stopped and instinctively glanced out the window at his pile of bricks.

"Oh, come on," she said, putting her arms around his neck. "We can use the charcoal grill this time. It'll be fun. Maybe Nathan will bring Katie."

After what had happened in the interrogation room yesterday, he seriously doubted that was going to happen. He looked down at his wife. She was all smiles this morning, and he was not about to say anything to change that.

"Okay?"

He sighed inwardly. Once she got an idea in her head, he knew it was going to stay there. Saying yes to her now, just meant peace of mind for him later. "Okay."

"Great. I'll buy everything at the grocery for it today." She walked him to the garage door and stood on her tiptoes to kiss him. "I love you."

He winked at her as he turned to go. "Love you, too."

~

The morning sun fell softly upon Nathan's face as he slept soundly next to Katie. She had been awake for a little while now and was watching him sleep. He lay on his side with his brown locks hanging down over his forehead. She resisted the urge to touch him as she felt this was the first good sleep he'd had in a long time.

Lance suddenly jumped up on the bed and announced, rather loudly, that he would like to have breakfast.

Nathan squinted open one eye and looked around. His eyes fell upon Katie as she sat scratching Lance between his ears.

"Good morning."

"Morning," he said, smiling. The sun's rays reflected all around her, highlighting her bare shoulders. He leaned over and kissed her softly, wishing that he could feel this way for the rest of his life.

~

Norma was sitting at her desk, studying her fingernails, when Nathan came through the door.

"Good morning, Norma."

She looked up in surprise. "Morning, Chief." In all the years she had known him, he had never taken the initiative to speak first.

"Any news on the cell number?"

"I've been on hold for twenty minutes now," she said, pointing to the receiver that was pressed against her ear.

"Okay," he said, smiling. "Let me know as soon as you get anything."

She watched him curiously as he walked into his office.

Jack and Hoskins came through the door at the same time. "Good morning, Norma."

"Morning, guys."

Hoskins poured himself a cup of coffee and glanced over his shoulder. "What's new?"

She switched the phone to her other ear and handed him two slips of paper. "Take your pick."

"Hmm..." he said, looking at each one. "I think I'll take the barking dog. Here, Collins."

Jack took the other piece of paper and read it. "No way! I've been to Mrs. Lenard's house *three* times this past week!"

Hoskins gave him a sly grin. "See ya later."

Jack scrambled after him and caught him by his sleeve. "I'll buy you lunch today if you take her this time."

He pursed his lips as if he were considering it. "Will you throw in dessert?"

"Don't push it."

"Have fun," he said, starting towards the door.

"All right, *fine!* I'll buy you dessert."

Si turned around and traded papers with him. "That's mighty nice of you, Collins."

Jack shook his head and smiled. "You *jerk*."

~

Katie wiped a bead of sweat off of her cheek as she leaned into the backseat of her car. She quickly began to regret her decision of putting icing on her brownies, as the ride over from the bakery had nearly melted them. She could only imagine what having them sit outside all afternoon was going to do.

Crystal Park was bustling with activity. Several vendors, like herself, were setting up their booths, which she noticed, ranged anywhere from elaborate, to unique. She couldn't help frowning when she looked at the plain folding table and chair she had brought.

She set the boxes down and headed back across the grass to get the rest. Over in the center of the park, hammers and drills could be heard as the stage was being assembled. Flyers had been posted all over town that Ricky Gunnar was going to be performing. She smiled inwardly, finding that she was looking forward to a free concert.

As she got to the sidewalk, she had to wait for several pedestrians to walk past her before she could open the car door.

"Here, let me help you with that." Nathan was suddenly by her side.

Katie let him take the boxes from her and leaned in to retrieve the last two from the backseat. "Thanks."

"How's your day been?"

"It's been a little hectic trying to get everything made and brought over here," she said, bumping the door closed with her hip.

"I like your t-shirt. It matches the color of your boxes."

She looked down at herself and laughed. She'd had a shirt printed with her logo on it last week. "Well, it's cheap advertising."

He followed her across the park and placed the boxes on the table.

"So, how's *your* day going?"

"Boring," he said, running his fingertips along her left hand. "I'd much rather be spending it with you."

Katie felt her heart race at his touch.

"Chief Sommers!"

He rolled his eyes. "I'll be right there!" he yelled over his shoulder.

"Sounds like you're needed," she said, giving him a smile. "I'll see you later."

He remained where he was. "Maybe afterwards, we can watch the fireworks together."

She nodded. "I'd like that."

Nathan took a slow and deliberate breath, finding that it was all he could do not to pull her into his arms and kiss her.

"Chief!"

He turned his head. "I'll be right there!"

"I better let you get to work," she said, brushing past him.

"Katie, wait."

She looked over her shoulder and saw that his expression had turned serious. "What's wrong?"

"There are going to be a lot of people here today. If you see anyone that's staring at you in a strange way, or if anybody comes up—"

"I'll let you know. I promise."

He suddenly took her by the hand and pulled her over behind a tree.

"What are you doing?" She giggled.

He glanced around quickly and then kissed her on the lips. After a moment, he drew back and smiled. "I'm sorry, but I just couldn't help myself."

She smiled back at him. "You can do that anytime you want."

~

The bra underneath Katie's t-shirt was soaked through with sweat. The heat was relentless, even though she was under the shade of a towering tree. She had served hundreds of people this afternoon and was down to her final three boxes.

All week, she had been looking forward to this day in hopes of boosting her name, as well as her sales. But right now, the only thing she wanted was to be in Nathan's arms. Vivid images from last night flashed in front of her.

"Enjoying the celebration?"

She looked up to see a man staring peculiarly at her.

"Excuse me?"

"You're smiling even though there's no one around."

Katie felt her face turning red.

"I'm sorry. I didn't mean to embarrass you." He stuck his hand out to her. "Malcolm Hodges. I'm a reporter for the paper. It's my job to be observant."

Although she didn't recognize his face, she definitely remembered his name and the way that Nathan had used it that day in her bakery. She nodded and shook his hand. "I believe we've met once before."

"You've got a good memory." He scratched the bottom of his beard and glanced around. "So, what do you think of our little town?"

There was something about him that she found disturbing. Maybe it was the way he was looking at her or the fact that his eyes kept dipping down upon her chest. Whatever the reason, it made her want to walk away. "It's starting to feel like home," she said, forcing a smile. Relief flooded her when she saw Jack heading her way.

"How's it going, Hodges?" he asked, slapping him on his back.

Mac seemed startled as he turned around. It took a moment for him to answer. "Good, Collins. How about you?"

"Can't complain."

"Any leads on the murders?"

"You know I can't comment on that," he said, trying to keep his voice friendly.

"How about off the record, then?"

Jack maintained his smile. "The mayor's about to give his speech. I'm sure you don't want to miss it."

"I think this town is more interested in the killer than they are the mayor's speech," he said, giving Katie a wink. "Don't you agree?"

Jack stepped in front of the table, blocking Katie from Hodges' view. "Have a good afternoon," he said pointedly.

Mac stared at him for a moment and then peered around his shoulder. "Nice talking with you again."

"You too," she said quietly.

"See ya around, Collins."

Jack watched him as he began weaving his way through the crowd.

"Thank you."

"No problem," he said, checking his watch. "I've got to get up front. Are you going to listen to the mayor's speech?"

The only thing she hated more than politics, were speeches. "Sure," she heard herself say, not wanting to be the odd man out. "I'll be over in a few minutes."

~

The Fourth of July in Silver Creek was always a huge turnout for both locals and tourists alike. Crystal Park served as the central hub for all the festivities. And it was no accident that it had been built right next to the lake. This gave politicians a captive audience during celebrations such as this.

Nathan stood in the grass with his back up against the left-hand side of the stage. Jack stood at the opposite end. Manning had always insisted that they be there, citing the need for security during public appearances like this.

Assassinations of mayors were rare, however, and he knew Manning was doing it just to make himself look important. Yet as he listened to him droning on, he found himself thinking that he wouldn't mind an attempted assassination.

The minutes slowly ticked by, and Nathan shifted his feet, wishing he would wrap things up. He was hot, thirsty, and tired of squinting into the sun. Out of the corner of his eye, he saw Hoskins making his way over to him.

His deputy put his hand on his shoulder and leaned in close. "There's something you need to see."

Nathan nodded and followed him around to the backside of the stage.

"Norma got the card to work and we've been going over the pictures." He cupped his hand over the top of the phone to shield it from the sun.

A photo popped up of Carol Fuqua standing beside a young man.

Hoskins pointed at the screen. "I've seen this kid before. He works at *Sam's*. He was the one who told me and Collins about Missy Rosenberg reserving the Jet Ski. His name's Jeremy Sanders."

Nathan recognized him as well. He remembered that he had lied to him about knowing Marissa Thomas. "All right. Let's go ask him a few questions." He turned to go and nearly smacked into Hodges.

"Where are you headed, *Chief*?"

A round of applause and whistles suddenly sounded, indicating that the mayor had finished his speech.

"I don't have time to talk right now," Nathan said, stepping around him.

Mac got in front of him, making him stop. "Has there been another murder?"

Nathan set his jaw. "Get out of my way, Hodges."

The crowd broke up and began meandering around them.

"Come on, Mac," Hoskins said, trying to defuse the situation, "let me buy you a burger."

Mac stood his ground.

Nathan leaned in close to him. "Don't do something you're going to regret."

"Oh, seriously? You're going to play the authority card on me?" Mac laughed as he looked around.

They now had the attention of several onlookers.

"Tell me something, *Chief.* Does your girlfriend know all your dirty little secrets?"

Nathan brought his fist back and hit him hard, knocking him to the ground.

Hoskins leaned over to help him up, but Mac waved him off. He slowly got to his knees and stood up. Blood dribbled from his lip and into his beard, making the injury look worse than it actually was.

Jack was suddenly there and put one hand against Nathan's chest. "What the *hell* are you doing?" he whispered.

Nathan glanced at the crowd of people. They stood with their mouths agape, horrified at what their chief of police had just done.

"Okay, folks. There's nothing to see here." Hoskins began moving them away.

Mac touched his lip with his fingers and looked at the bright red blood. He lunged towards Nathan, but Jack stepped in front of him.

The mayor pushed his way through the spectators and strode up to Nathan. When he spoke, his voice was just above a whisper. "I want you in my office in *ten* minutes."

The loudspeaker suddenly crackled. "Ladies and Gentlemen, if you'll take your seats, Ricky Gunnar is about to take the stage."

A round of cheers suddenly went up as the crowd began to disperse.

Nathan turned away and began walking towards his truck. He briefly caught sight of Katie standing in the midst of all the people. She looked embarrassed for him.

~

Manning's staff had the day off, which made his office unusually quiet. Nathan leaned his head back against the cushion of the long leather couch as he waited.

The floor beneath his feet vibrated softly from the band playing in the park. He drew in a deep breath and sighed, wishing that Manning would hurry up. It had been over forty-five minutes. Prolonging his execution was just plain cruel.

His right hand began to throb as it gripped the arm of the sofa. Glancing down, he noticed that he had reopened the gash on his knuckles.

The door suddenly swung open, making him sit up.

Manning walked inside with his cell phone pressed against his ear. "I'm going to deal with it as quietly as possible," he said, looking around the room until he spied Nathan on the couch. "I'll talk to you Monday. Have a good weekend."

Nathan braced himself for the fallout.

"Well, you've really outdone yourself this time, Sommers," Manning said, shaking his head. "What the *hell* were you thinking?"

Knowing there really wasn't anything he could say to make him happy, he chose to remain silent.

"I've just spent the last half hour trying to talk Malcolm Hodges out of pressing charges against you."

"He was interfering with police business."

"So you *hit* him?"

"I'm sorry...I let him get under my skin. I'll apologize to him."

"It's a little late for apologies. It's bad enough that we have these *goddamn* murders hanging over our heads. Then you have to go and pull a stunt like this!"

Nathan got to his feet. "I'm sorry, Tom. I never meant to cause you any embarrassment."

"It's not that simple. You punched a guy in front of dozens of people. I can't just look the other way." He held up his cell phone. "Do you know how many calls I've gotten in the last half hour from members of the city council? I don't know what the *hell* to tell them."

"I'm sure you'll think of something," he replied, unable to keep the sarcasm out of his tone.

"You just don't get it, do you? Your actions are a direct reflection on *me!*"

Nathan felt his anger returning. "And we all know how precious your reputation is, don't we, Tom?"

Manning clenched his jaw. "Malcolm Hodges is with your deputy right now filing a formal complaint against you. An investigation into the incident will be conducted. But for now, you're suspended until further notice."

Nathan stared at him, not believing what he was hearing. "We're in the middle of a *murder* investigation. You can't do this!"

"Give me your badge."

"Come on, Tom."

Manning held out his hand. "Your badge," he repeated.

Nathan unclipped his shield from his belt and tossed it on his desk. "This is not right, and *you*

239

know it." He turned around and headed towards the door.

Manning lowered his hand. "Nathan?"

He stopped but didn't turn around.

"I strongly suggest you consider handing in your resignation."

~

Katie stood under the shower, letting the cool water run over her. After what had happened this afternoon, she hadn't felt like staying for the concert. She'd packed up the remaining brownies from her table and driven straight home.

She hadn't actually seen Nathan hit Mac Hodges but had heard all about it from several spectators. She found herself not knowing *what* to think about the incident, but it had left her with an odd feeling.

As she dried herself off, Lance came through the door and greeted her. "Hi, sweetie." She bent down and scratched his head before making her way into the bedroom.

She picked up her cell phone off the nightstand, hoping that Nathan had called while she was in the shower. She frowned upon seeing that there were no messages.

~

Jack banged loudly on Nathan's front door until he finally opened it.

"I don't want any company right now."

He pushed past him.

Nathan sighed and dropped his hand. "By all means, come in."

"Hodges filed a complaint against you."

"I heard."

"What happened today?"

Nathan walked over and sat down on his sofa.

"I can't help you unless you tell me what happened."

"I don't need, or *want,* your help right now, Jack," he said, picking up his bottle of beer from the coffee table.

Nathan's cell phone rang, echoing off the walls of the now silent room.

He reached into his pocket and glanced at the screen. Seeing it was Katie, he ignored it.

Jack sat down beside him and looked at him expectantly.

Nathan knew he wasn't going to leave until he got an answer. "What happened was between me and Hodges," he said, being in no mood to give him one.

"Not anymore. Now it's going to become public. Is that what you want?"

"*No,* that's not what I *want!* But I don't have a choice anymore, do I?"

"Does this have something to do with Jenny?"

Nathan suddenly leaned forward and held his head in his hands. Tonight, the mere mention of her name brought him to the verge of tears.

"I know you feel responsible for her death," Jack said, placing a hand on his shoulder, "but it wasn't your fault."

"You don't understand, Jack," he said, keeping his face buried in his hands.

"I understand *enough.*"

He slowly lifted his head.

"I understand that she's dead and that no amount of guilt, or shame, is going to bring her back. And I *swear,* Nathan, sometimes you act as if you're dead, too. Look around you," he said, gesturing with his hand. "This place is like a shrine. You *have* to get on with your life."

"That's really easy for you to say, *Jack,*" he said bitterly. "You've gotten everything you ever wanted."

Guilt flooded his deputy's face, making him look away.

Nathan tilted his head back and took a long and deliberate swallow of his beer. When he was done, he wiped the edges of his mouth. "Manning asked me for my resignation."

"What did you tell him?"

He sighed and ran his fingers through his hair.

"So, just like that. You're gonna leave—"

"This has been coming for a long time now, Jack." He stood up and walked around the table. "It was a mistake for me to have stayed here."

"What about Katie?"

He finished what was left in his bottle and shrugged.

"I saw you with her at the park today," Jack said, getting to his feet. "You both seemed really happy."

"She's better off without me."

Jack strode over to where he was standing. "*You* listen to me," he said, tapping his finger against his chest. "What happened to Jenny and the baby was unfair. But you can't live with their *ghosts*, Nathan!"

He began walking away, not wanting to hear anymore.

Jack grabbed him by the arm, forcing him to look at him. "Do you hear me? She would *not* want you living like this!"

Nathan suddenly jerked away from his grasp as everything he'd been holding inside for the past two years came rushing to the surface. "I *cheated* on her, Jack!" He turned and hurled the bottle across the room, shattering the window above the kitchen sink. His mouth twisted in agony as he looked back at him. "I *cheated* on Jenny! Hodges found out and sent her pictures. *That's* what we argued about that night! She drove off upset, and *that's* why she's *dead!*"

Jack was silent for a long time. Then very slowly, he began to shake his head. "You *son-of-a-bitch*." He grabbed him by his shirt and shook him. "How could you do that to her? She was *pregnant* for Christ's sake!"

A jagged sob tore loose from Nathan's throat.

"Was it with that girl at my wedding?"

The only answer Nathan could give him was another sob.

He shook him again. *"Was it?"*

"Yes," he whispered.

Jack drew his fist back and hit him squarely on the left side of his cheek.

The force of the blow sent him to the floor.

He stood over him with his fists clenched. "I don't *fucking* believe you, Nathan! I don't *fucking* believe you!" He turned and stormed out, kicking the screen door on his way.

Chapter Twenty-two

It was after nine by the time Jack got to the marina. He breathed a sigh of relief when he saw that the lights were still on inside *Sam's*.

His thoughts remained on Nathan as he stepped out of his truck and began making his way down the deserted ramp. Most everyone by now was either anchored out on the lake, or milling about Crystal Park, waiting for the fireworks to start.

He pulled on the front door but found it locked. Peering inside, he could see Sam Bryant standing behind the register. He rapped on the glass to get his attention.

Bryant looked over and held up a finger in acknowledgment.

Jack shifted his feet impatiently as he waited for him to come around the counter and unlock the door.

"What are you doing here this time of night, Collins?"

He sighed as he tried to push Nathan to the back of his mind. "Sorry to bother you, Sam. I know you're trying to close up, but I was wondering if I could speak with Jeremy Sanders for a minute."

Bryant turned his head, revealing his trademark ponytail. "Hey, Sanders!" he called in a gruff voice. "Get out here for a minute!" He took a step back, as he motioned for Jack to come inside.

"How's business?"

"It's *always* good on the Fourth," Bryant answered with a smile.

Jack heard movement in the back and then a young man in a red t-shirt and board shorts appeared in the doorway behind the register.

"Yeah?" he said, looking at Sam.

Bryant jerked his thumb over his shoulder. "Deputy Collins wants to talk to you."

Sanders walked slowly around the counter.

"Did you know Carol Fuqua?" Jack asked, pulling out his notepad.

He hesitated a moment and then shrugged. "She was that bank teller. The first girl that was killed, right?"

"Did you know her personally?"

The healthy tan Sanders sported began to drain from his face. "Why are you asking me that?"

He tilted his head. "It's a simple question, son."

The Adam's apple in Sanders' throat bobbed up and down as he looked over his shoulder.

Jack followed his gaze.

Bryant had gone back behind the register and was checking the receipt totals. He didn't appear to be paying any attention to what was being said.

"Did you?" he repeated.

Sanders' eyes darted about as he shifted his weight to his other foot.

Jack put his notepad away and rested his hand on his Glock. This seemed to make the kid even more nervous. He lowered his hand and tried a different approach. "Can I see your cell phone?"

"Why do you need to see my phone?"

"Okay, here's the deal," Jack said, growing irritated. "You can either answer my questions *here*, or you can answer them at the station house. It's your choice."

Sanders reluctantly reached into his front pocket and handed him the phone.

Jack flipped it open and checked his incoming calls against the victim's number. They were a match. "Carol Fuqua made several calls to you over the last two months before she was killed." He watched him closely as he continued. "Were you seeing her?"

Bryant stopped tallying up the receipts and looked over their way. He peered at Sanders over the rim of his glasses but didn't say anything. It seemed that he too was waiting for his answer.

"We'd been dating for a couple of months," he finally said.

"The last call she made to you was at four in the afternoon on the day she died. Do you remember what it was about?"

"We were supposed to meet here later that day and go out on my friend's boat. She called to tell me she was running a little late."

"What time did you see her?"

He shook his head. "She never showed up. I tried calling her, but she didn't answer."

"What did you do next?"

"I met up with some of my buddies on the boardwalk. We went over to *The Game Zone* and played some pool."

"You weren't concerned about your girlfriend?"

"No. I just figured she'd changed her mind."

"Why didn't you tell the police any of this?"

"Because I was afraid you'd think I killed her." His face suddenly showed just how much of a frightened kid he was. "I swear to you, I didn't. I would never hurt her."

"Can anybody verify you were at *The Game Zone* the night she was murdered?"

Sanders stared at the wooden floor for a moment and then nodded excitedly. "I've got a card stamp," he said, reaching into his back pocket. "For every ten games I play, I get one free." He handed a crinkled card to Jack and pointed. "See? There's the date and time. We played three games."

Jack studied it for a moment as he checked the dates.

"Dave is the manager. He can tell you I was there that night. I played a round with him and lost—had to pay him twenty bucks."

"I'm going to need you to come down to the station first thing in the morning," Jack said, handing it back to him, "and give a signed statement to what you just told me. Understand?"

Relief, mixed with anxiety, flooded his eyes. "Can I go now?"

"Yeah."

Sanders looked over at Bryant, seeking his approval as well.

"Go on," Bryant said, waving him off. "I'll see you tomorrow."

He stepped around Jack, giving him a wide berth, and hurried out the door.

"Geez, Collins, you had that poor boy about to piss in his pants."

Jack couldn't help feeling disappointed as he made his way over to the counter. "How long has he worked for you?"

"About four months now, I guess."

"How well do you know him?"

Sam shook his head and smiled. "He's a good kid. He wouldn't harm a flea."

Jack watched as he recorded the receipts. "Can you give me his home address?"

He dropped the pen and sighed. "Sure. I'll be right back."

Jack's cell phone rang as Bryant went into the back room. A twinge of fear came over him when he saw it was Cheryl. "Is everything all right?"

"I'm fine. But where are you? It's getting late."

"I'm at the marina," he replied, checking his watch. "I should be home in about half an hour."

"Okay. But would you stop and bring me home some ice cream?"

"Absolutely," he said, amused by his wife's late-night cravings. Movement caught his eye as he saw Sam return from the back with a file. "What flavor?"

"Mmm...I think I'm in the mood for some chocolate cherry jubilee."

"Chocolate cherry jubilee. All right, woman," he said, grinning. "I'll see what I can do." He watched as Sam began scribbling down the address for him.

"Love you."

His smile suddenly faded. "Love you, too." He slid the phone into his pocket.

"Here you go." Sam held out a piece of paper to him.

"Thanks." He looked at it for a moment before tucking it in his shirt pocket. "You know, I couldn't help noticing when you were doing your receipts that you were using your right hand. But just now, you were writing with your left."

Sam stared at him curiously and then laughed. "I'm left-handed, but my parents taught me to write with my other hand. They said it would be easier on me. I learned to use both pretty good."

Jack nodded as he casually glanced around. His eyes caught on the frogs in the display shelf to his right. He took a step closer and peered down at them. Housed in glass jars, they were suspended in some sort of liquid resin. "Do people really want to buy dead frogs?"

"You'd be surprised what these tourists will buy," he said, walking around the register. "I sell about ten of these guys a week." He stopped and looked at his watch. "I'm thinking about going and hunting for some tonight—that is—if I ever get out of here."

Jack watched his mannerisms as he talked. He was relaxed and chatty like he always was, but there was something in his voice that sounded strange.

"Have you ever gone gigging, Collins?"

"No."

Sam took off his glasses and let them fall around his neck. "It's a lot of fun. You should come with me sometime. Here," he said, leaning over the counter. "Let me show you what I use."

Jack quietly unsnapped his holster and slipped his hand around the grip.

After a moment, Bryant straightened up and held out a small metal instrument to him. "This is my pride and joy," he said, beaming. "I made it myself."

He carefully took the gig from Sam's fingers. It had a long handle and was u-shaped. It was different from any he'd ever seen, having only two tines instead of three, and spaced about three inches apart. His heart began to pound.

"Do you like it?"

"Yeah," he half-whispered.

Sam slid his hands in his pockets and grinned. "They're not hard to make. You see that long handle gives me lots of leverage. It pierces their skin very easily."

Jack tightened his grip around his Glock and started to pull it out.

In less time than it took to blink, Sam pulled out a switchblade and thrust it deep inside him.

Jack's mouth opened, but nothing came out except a gasp for air.

Bryant put his right hand on Jack's shoulder as he pushed the knife farther in with his left. "Sorry, Collins."

The gig fell from Jack's fingers as he dropped to his knees.

With a quick jerk, Bryant pulled the blade out.

Jack's hands instinctively moved to where the knife had been. He made a gurgling sound as the blood spilled from between his lips.

Bryant put his boot in the middle of his chest and pushed him backward. He then straddled him with his feet and brought the knife close to his face. "I'm really sorry, Collins," he said, cutting the cord to his mic.

Unable to move, Jack watched helplessly as Bryant stripped him of his gun and cell phone, before turning out the lights and locking the door.

Jack's breathing grew shallow as the blood seeped through his fingers. His thoughts immediately turned to Cheryl, and the daughter that he would never know. In his mind, he already knew what she was going to look like. She would be every bit as beautiful as her mother, inside and out.

Something warm began trickling down his cheek but he couldn't lift his hands. As the blood drained from his body, he closed his eyes and dreamed of Cheryl. He could hear the fireworks booming overhead as darkness surrounded him.

~

Nathan sat on the edge of his bed staring at the wall. In the back of his mind, he'd always hoped that confessing what he had done would somehow bring him peace.

He tenderly touched the side of his face. But atonement hadn't come.

The phone on his nightstand rang, shattering the silence around him. Ignoring it, he reached for the piece of paper lying beside it. The words he had written were short and to the point. His resignation would make it easier on everyone, including himself.

His phone had no sooner stopped ringing than his cell phone started. Nathan sighed as he looked at the screen. It was Cheryl. "Hello?"

"Nathan? I'm worried about Jack."

"What's wrong?" he asked, sitting forward.

"I spoke to him a while ago and he said he was at the marina. He told me he was on his way home. But that was almost an hour ago."

He rubbed the back of his neck. "He probably just got another call, Cheryl. I'm sure it's nothing to worry about."

"Don't patronize me because I'm pregnant, Nathan! I know something's wrong, I can *feel* it! He's not answering his cell, and I can't raise him on our scanner. He would have called me if he'd gotten delayed."

"Did you try Hoskins?"

"*Yes*, I tried Hoskins!"

Nathan held the phone away from his ear as she raised her voice another decibel.

"He's not answering either!"

He stood up and clipped his holster to his belt. "I'm on my way to the marina now," he said, reaching for his keys. "I'll call you."

~

Nathan passed several trucks with boat trailers headed in the other direction as he sped towards the marina.

He held the walkie-talkie to his mouth. "Hoskins? What's your 10-20?" There was no chatter on the radio tonight. It was oddly quiet. "Collins, what's your location?"

He laid the radio on the seat beside him and tried both deputies on their cells. Neither one answered.

He rounded the curve that led to the boat docks and slowed down. Jack's truck was parked near the ramp. He pulled up behind it and grabbed his radio and flashlight before climbing out.

His hands felt along the hood of Jack's truck. It was cold. A sense of alarm came over him as he quickly scanned the parking lot. The light posts shed just enough brightness for him to see that there was no one here.

He started to head down the ramp but stopped and went back to his truck. He opened the glove compartment and pulled out a small holster containing his Glock 27. It was much smaller than his 23 and easier to conceal. He used to carry a backup gun when he was on the force in Sacramento but found that there was rarely a need for it here in Silver Creek. He clipped it to his belt behind his back and hurried towards the marina.

He walked briskly along the pier, stopping to check each door. They were all locked tight, including *Sam's*.

A man's voice, followed by laughter, made him spin around. He squinted into the darkness and saw a couple exiting the gate. They were unaware of his presence as they groped and kissed each other on their way to the parking lot.

He turned and walked around the side of the building to check the back door. A boat creaked softly behind him as it pulled against its cleat.

Static came across his radio.

"This is Hoskins, Chief. Go ahead."

He unclipped his radio and pushed the button. "What's your 10-20?"

"I'm over at the jail. Had to haul in a DWI. Sorry, I had my radio turned off and didn't realize it."

"Did Collins tell you why he was going to the marina tonight?"

"Yeah. He was going down there to question the Sanders kid. Why?"

Nathan looked at the radio and knew Cheryl was probably listening. "Stand by." He clipped it back on his belt and walked around to the front of Bryant's store again. Where the *hell* was he? His footsteps faltered when he noticed a small dark spot directly in front of the door. He knew what it was before touching it with his fingertips.

Drawing his gun, he hugged the side of the building and crept around to the rear door. He counted to three and kicked it in, ducking inside as it slammed against the wall.

He moved silently past the storage room, his adrenaline rushing through him. "Collins?" He leaned against the doorway and slipped behind the register. He moved his flashlight left to right in a sweeping motion, keeping his other hand on the trigger of his gun. The light suddenly caught something and he brought it back.

Jack's lifeless body lay on the floor a few feet away.

Nathan stumbled around the counter and knelt beside him. There was so much blood that he couldn't tell where he was bleeding from. He shook him gently. "Jack!"

The hot sting of tears began to form as Nathan cradled him in his arms. He spread his fingers across his chest and shook him again. "Collins!"

Jack's eyelids slowly fluttered open.

Nathan held him tight, trying to will his own life into his. "Who did this?"

Jack's breath rattled as he fought hard for the next one. "Sam," he whispered.

~

Nathan watched silently through the emergency room doors as the doctors and nurses surrounded Jack. He lay unmoving on the stretcher as they hooked him up to tubes and machines.

"Nathan!"

He began to tremble inside when he saw Cheryl running towards him. He caught her by the shoulders and forced her to take three steps backward.

A small cry escaped her as she looked at his shirt.

He glanced down at himself and saw that he was covered in Jack's blood.

"Is he all right?" she asked, clutching at his arms.

"The doctors are with him now."

"What happened? Si won't tell me!"

Looking past her, he caught sight of Hoskins who had brought her here.

"Tell me!"

Nathan tightened his jaw. "He was stabbed."

Cheryl searched his face, her eyes begging him to tell her that he was going to be okay.

"I'm sorry," he whispered.

She suddenly pushed against him. "I need to see him!"

"You can't right now."

"I need to see him—"

"Cheryl, no."

"I need to see him."

She began to struggle so much that Nathan had to let go for fear of hurting her.

"Mrs. Collins?" A man with thinning black hair and a haggard face stood solemnly in front of the emergency room doors.

"How is he?" she asked, stepping around Nathan.

"The knife perforated your husband's liver. We're taking him to surgery now to try and stop the bleeding."

"Is he going to be all right?"

The doctor gave Nathan a subtle glance before answering her. "He's lost a lot of blood. But we're going to do everything we can." His words sounded rigid and rehearsed as he turned and hurried towards the elevator.

Cheryl's body began to convulse with sobs causing her legs to buckle underneath her.

Nathan lunged forward and caught her in his arms.

"I can't lose him, Nathan!" She buried her face in his shoulder. "I can't lose him...I can't..."

As he held her against him, he suddenly felt the life inside of her move. "I know," he whispered.

Hoskins turned away and wiped his eyes.

Nathan led her over to a small waiting area and eased her down into a chair.

Continuous sobs rolled out of her mouth as she held her head in her hands.

He knelt in front of her. "Cheryl, look at me," he said in a stern, but gentle voice.

After a moment, she slowly raised her eyes to meet his.

"I know this is hard, but you have to calm down. You need to think about the baby."

She shook her head, unleashing a long stream of tears. "He is my *life*, Nathan! I can't live without him. *I can't!*"

Si sat down beside her and put his big arm across her shoulders. "Jack's not going anywhere, Cheryl. You know as well as I do that he's too stubborn to die."

Something between a laugh and a cry fell from her lips.

"He's gonna be just fine," he whispered reassuringly.

Cheryl nodded as she leaned against him.

Nathan stood up and walked out of the waiting room, motioning for Hoskins to follow.

Si said a few more words of encouragement to her before getting to his feet. When he was out of earshot, he turned to Nathan. "What do you need me to do, Boss?"

"I want you to pull Bryant's picture from the DMV, and put out a BOLO on him and his vehicle," he said, walking quickly down the corridor towards the exit. "Alert the border and neighboring counties. I want them to set up roadblocks, and check every car that comes through." He paused at the top of the steps that led to the parking lot. "Tell them that he is armed and considered dangerous."

"You got it, Boss," he said, hurrying down the steps. On his way out, he brushed past the mayor.

Nathan turned and began walking back towards the ER. Manning was the last person he wanted to see right now.

"Sommers? What the heck is going on?"

He quickened his pace making Manning have to run to catch up to him.

Tom grabbed his arm and turned him, but his expression softened when he saw his face. "What happened?"

Nathan glanced over at Cheryl. She was sitting with her head bowed against her chest as she slowly rocked herself back and forth.

Manning followed his gaze and then lowered his voice. "My aide called and told me that Collins had been stabbed."

Nathan's eyes suddenly welled up. It seemed that he had lost control of everything right now, including his emotions.

"Who stabbed him?"

"Sam Bryant. He's our killer," he said, wiping his eyes on the sleeve of his shirt.

Manning stared at him in disbelief.

"Hoskins is putting out a BOLO right now, and we're coordinating roadblocks at the border and neighboring counties." He turned to leave, but Manning put his hand out.

"Where are you going?"

Nathan clenched his jaw. "I'm going to go find the *son-of-a-bitch*."

"Then you're going to need this," he said, reaching into his pocket.

Nathan looked down and saw his badge.

"If you need anything, call me."

He gave him a nod before running down the steps. The double doors slid open as he reached for his cell and dialed Katie's number.

After four rings, she picked up. "Hello?"

"It's me."

Katie sat up in bed, hearing the strangeness in his voice. "What's wrong?"

"Can you come down to the hospital?"

"What's happened? Are you all right?"

He closed his eyes for a moment and took a deep breath. "Jack's been stabbed. It doesn't look good—" He stopped and gripped the phone tighter in an attempt to stop what was coming up.

"I'm so sorry, Nathan."

"Cheryl could really use a friend."

Katie held the phone against her shoulder as she slipped on a pair of jeans. "I can be there in ten minutes."

"Thank you."

Her doorbell rang as she stepped into her shoes. "Hold on a sec. There's someone at my door." She hurried into the living room and turned on the lamp. "Who is it?"

"It's Deputy Hoskins. The chief sent me to check on you."

"Katie?" Nathan asked impatiently.

"It's Si," she said into the phone as she unlocked the door.

Nathan's face turned from confusion to fear when he saw Hoskins parked alongside the curb in front of him. "Katie, don't open the door! Do you hear me? *Don't open the door!*"

He ran for his truck and motioned for Hoskins to follow. "Katie!"

He heard a lot of commotion and something that sounded like a whimper. Then nothing but silence.

"Katie!"

~

Four and a half minutes later, Nathan screeched into Katie's driveway. By the time Hoskins pulled up, he was already at her front door. He pointed for him to go around back.

His deputy nodded and drew his weapon.

The door stood slightly ajar as Nathan pushed it open with the tip of his gun. His eyes quickly scanned the room. "Katie!"

He heard Hoskins kick in the back door. "Clear!"

"Search the bedrooms!"

As his deputy went to check, Nathan saw Katie's cell phone lying on the carpet by his foot. He knelt down to retrieve it and saw a shadow out of the corner of his eye.

"Meow!" Lance slunk out from underneath the couch and began to rub hard against his leg.

"Clear!" called Hoskins from the hallway.

Nathan slid his gun in his holster.

Hoskins met him in the living room. "No sign of Bryant. But that's his Jeep parked out front," he said, holstering his weapon. "He must have taken her car."

He nodded as he stood up and looked around. Katie's purse and keys were on the floor next to an overturned lamp. He ran his fingers through his hair as if that would help to clear his mind.

Hoskins, his ever-faithful deputy, stood poised and ready for the next order.

The weight of everything suddenly fell upon Nathan, crushing him as he fell back against the wall. He bent over and placed his hands on his knees as he fought to get a deep breath.

Hoskins awkwardly placed his hand on his shoulder. "It's okay, Boss. We're going to find her." After a moment, he removed his hand and waited.

Nathan remained where he was.

"I'm going to send out a broadcast that Bryant may have a hostage, and I'll put out a description of Katie and her car."

Nathan closed his eyes and nodded as Hoskins stepped outside. Everything that had unfolded in the last hour seemed surreal. Sam Bryant was a long-standing member of the community, liked by everyone.

He felt himself start to shake as he clenched and unclenched his fists. He had been right in front of him the entire time.

"Boss!"

He straightened up and went out the door.

"Just came over the wire that a state trooper reported seeing a car fitting our description about ten minutes ago heading north on 253."

~

It was nearly two in the morning when Nathan reached the roadblock near Scobey in Daniels County. He pulled over to the side and flashed his badge at the trooper. "Chief Sommers."

The state trooper offered him his hand. "Mattingly. Come on over here, we'll show you where we are."

Nathan followed the officer over to his squad car. A map was spread out on top of the hood with a rock placed at each corner to keep it from blowing away.

The trooper held a flashlight over it for him to see. "This is where we are," he said, pointing at the red circle. "The victim's car was last spotted here."

Nathan leaned closer and studied the map. The car had not been seen since the first BOLO was put out. It had also not been positively identified as Katie's. They were just grasping at straws at this point.

"We've got roadblocks set up every ten miles between here and Coronach. And we've done the same east towards Flaxville, Redstone, and then up to Raymond."

"There aren't many side roads between here and the Canadian border," Nathan said.

Mattingly shook his head. "No. If he wants to cross by car, he's going to have to do it here. Now, there's always the possibility that he's cut over and is intending to cross at Whitetail."

Nathan grimaced. It would be easy to gain entry through there since Big Beaver, one of Canada's checkpoints, had closed earlier last year.

"We've got a chopper in the air searching this area." He circled the map with his finger. "Including the side roads headed northeast towards Whitetail. It's just a matter of time before we find him."

Nathan noticed the confidence in his voice. He wished he felt that way, too, but at this point, they weren't even sure if he had come this way. He knew that once Bryant crossed the border he would be extremely difficult to find. He could easily get to a town and slip away unnoticed.

Mattingly reached through the window of his car and retrieved a thermos. "You look like you could use a hot cup of coffee."

"Thanks." Nathan leaned against the car and took a sip as the trooper watched.

"So this guy Bryant...is he the one that's killed all those women?"

"We believe he is," he replied. An anxious sigh fell from him as he took another sip of coffee. Now came the hard part of waiting.

He could not even begin to think about the hell Katie must be going through. The one thing that gave him hope was the fact that Bryant needed her. He needed her to cross the border. His stomach began to churn as he checked his watch. Time was running out. Nathan knew that once he got across, he would be done with her.

Chapter Twenty-three

Katie's head lay back against the seat as she stared out her window. She focused on the white line on the edge of the road, making sure to keep her eyes away from her abductor.

When she had opened her front door earlier tonight, she'd expected to find Si Hoskins standing on the other side. Instead, a man she had never seen before forced his way in and overpowered her. He had then bound her hands behind her back and dragged her outside, all the while holding a knife against her throat.

A wave of fear suddenly took hold of her. She bit down on the inside of her cheek, trying desperately not to cry as the rational part of her mind told her that the best thing to do was remain calm.

They passed another mile marker. She turned her head slightly in order to see the clock on the dashboard. It read two twenty-one. They had been driving for just over three hours now. She tried wiggling her fingers but couldn't. The tape was wrapped around her wrists so tightly that she'd lost all feeling in them.

The car suddenly slowed and veered sharply off the road.

She watched as he shut off the headlights and looked up. A bright, moving light descended from the sky. It swept back and forth along the road as it headed in their direction. Filled with hope, she immediately sat forward.

The man swiveled his head towards her. "Don't move." His voice was deep, and matter-of-fact, nothing like she thought it would be.

Katie could now see the underbelly of the helicopter as it drew closer. If she could just get out of the car, the road was only about ten feet away.

She glanced at her captor. At the moment, he was preoccupied with the helicopter. She pivoted her legs to the left so that her back was partially against the passenger's side door. Her numb fingers felt frantically along the panel for the handle. She grasped at it and pulled, only to realize that he had locked the door.

He heard the click of the handle as she released it and turned sharply to look at her. Reaching down, he grabbed the knife beside his leg.

Katie's eyes focused on the blade as he brought it near her face. She leaned away from it until the back of her head hit the window.

He pressed the side of it to her throat. "I *said*, 'Don't move.'"

The light from the helicopter was right beside the car now.

He held the blade against her as he turned once more to look at the chopper.

Katie watched helplessly as the beam moved farther and farther away.

He removed the knife from her throat and brandished it in front of her. She could see from its tip down to the handle that it was coated in dried blood.

He tilted his head sideways at her. "You seem like a smart girl. But what you did just now was stupid, and stupid girls get killed." He put the edge of the blade to her bottom lip.

She took in her breath as he pushed it against her.

Slowly, he moved it down her lip, following the contour of her chin.

She felt him turn the knife on its end and press the pointed tip into her skin. "Please..." she whispered.

He pushed harder until it broke through, causing her to cry out. He briefly closed his eyes and breathed in. "Do you know that I can smell your fear? It's right...*there*," he said, pressing the blade directly under her chin. "Just underneath your skin. It oozes out of your pores as your adrenaline rushes."

Katie watched his eyes grow black as he breathed in again. They were so dark she couldn't see his pupils. He was like a being with no soul.

"That bank teller had the strongest scent. She was my first." He grinned as if thinking back. "Well, the first one I signed my name to."

She tried to recoil as he turned the knife on its side and let it glide along her throat.

He raked it across her chest, stopping just above her left breast. "She was a shy girl," he said as he began caressing it with the blade. "I figured she might take to the attention I paid her, but she didn't want anything to do with me."

He suddenly put his other hand around the back of her neck. His fingers squeezed hard as he leaned in close. "I'll let you in on a little secret, Katie." He stopped and glanced around as if he were pretending that people were listening. "She screamed the loudest of all of them. Right up until the end," he whispered. "She begged me not to kill her, said she would do *anything*. But you know what?" He shook his head and sighed. "It was too late for that. I'm sort of a first impression type of guy, Katie." He pressed the knife against her throat again as he bent down towards her chest.

She closed her eyes and fought back the tears as he began kissing her breasts, his tongue dipping inside her cleavage. The scruff of his goatee grated across her chest like sandpaper.

He drew back and looked up at her. "What about *you*, Katie? Would you do anything to live?"

Her breathing was ragged, laced with suppressed sobs. She didn't want to answer him.

He slowly lowered the knife. "Sit back."

Tears flowed down her face as she did as he instructed.

He pressed on the accelerator and pulled back onto the road.

~

Si knelt beside the puddle of blood inside Bryant's store. He tried to shut his emotions off as best he could, but found it to be an impossible task.

He leaned over and picked up what appeared to be a frog gig a few feet from where the blood was. He placed it inside a baggie and stood up.

Bryant's store was filled to the brim with merchandise. The walls were lined with kayaks, canoes, and oars, while the rows of shelves held everything from fishing lures to tampons.

He moved behind the register to the storage room. There was a lot more merchandise, still in boxes, that filled the small space.

Si walked down one side and then the other, stopping to check in some of the cartons. He paused for a moment when he came to three very large boxes. They were stacked one on top of the other from floor to ceiling. There was nothing out of the ordinary about them, except for the fact that there were some scuff marks on the floor in front of them. The marks were in the shape of an arc, as if the boxes had been swung out, and then back.

Hoskins placed his hands on the bottom one and pushed them away from the wall. They were heavy, and it took all his strength to move them. A padlocked door was suddenly exposed.

He rushed to the front of the store to retrieve a hammer he'd remembered seeing on one of the shelves. When he returned, he hit the lock full force and jerked open the door.

A long string, attached to a single light bulb, dangled above his head. A pull on it lit up the small closet. He let his eyes wander around the space. Several brown plastic bottles lined the floor beside a wooden chair. Si felt a wave of nausea as he saw the blood spatters on the wall. *"That sick bastard."*

~

Nathan watched the drops of rain begin to cover his windshield. What had started out as a light shower had quickly turned into a downpour, forcing him to take refuge inside the cab of his truck.

Being confined only made his anxiety worse with each passing minute. Of course, the six cups of coffee he'd drunk wasn't helping matters. Mattingly had given him his thermos, telling him he needed it more than he did.

The sound of his cell phone ringing nearly caused him to jump out of his skin. Grabbing it off the dash, he looked at the screen before answering. "Go ahead, Hoskins."

"Boss, I'm at the marina inside Bryant's store. I think I've found the murder weapon that he used on the victims."

He listened as Hoskins described the frog gig, along with the findings in the closet.

"Bryant probably used the ether to subdue them long enough to get them inside. Based on the amount of blood in here, I'd say this is where he killed them."

An involuntary shudder went through Nathan as he thought about Katie being with him.

"Wibaux County is sending me one of their forensics guys. They should be here in a few hours. I'm headed over to search Bryant's residence now."

Nathan rubbed his forehead. "Keep me posted, Si."

"Will do, Boss."

"Any news on Collins?"

There was nothing but silence on the other end for a long time. "He's out of surgery, but that's all I know. Norma's at the hospital with Cheryl. She said she would call me if anything happens."

Nathan knew by the hesitation in his voice that he wasn't telling him everything. "Okay, I'll wait to hear from you."

As he hung up, he felt the guilt creeping in. His actions today had set off a chain of events that could never be undone.

He started to call the hospital but saw he had a voice mail waiting. His heart rose when he saw it was Katie's number, but immediately fell when he noticed the time stamp. She must have left the message when Jack had been over at his house earlier this evening.

His hand trembled as he held the phone to his ear. "Nathan, it's Katie. I just wanted to talk with you for a little while and make sure that you were all right. Please call me…it doesn't matter how late it is." There was a slight pause. "I also wanted to tell you how much I enjoyed being with you last night. I'll talk to you soon. 'Bye."

Nathan rested his head against the steering wheel and closed his eyes. This morning was a new beginning for him. It was the first time in two years that he hadn't woke up thinking of Jenny. His emotions came rushing to the surface, causing his entire body to shake.

~

Cheryl stood beside the hospital bed holding Jack's hand in her own. About an hour ago, he had been put on a ventilator to help his breathing. She watched as the black accordion-like instrument rose and fell in rhythm with his chest.

Heavy blood loss had caused him to go into shock during the surgery. The surgeon had told her that the next twelve hours were going to be the most critical for him. Further complicating matters were his kidneys, which were already showing signs of stress.

She reached out and swept his blond locks from his forehead, wishing with all of her heart that he would open his eyes.

The baby suddenly kicked.

Fresh tears began to fall down her cheeks as she took his hand in hers and placed it against her stomach. "Jack, I can't do this by myself. Please don't leave me." She bent down and kissed the side of his face. "I love you so much."

"Cheryl?"

She recognized Norma's voice but didn't turn around.

"Why don't you come with me to the cafeteria?"

She shook her head. "I can't leave him."

The older woman put her arm around her. "I understand. But you have to take care of yourself."

"I am."

Norma started to say something but stopped. There was no point. She knew she wasn't going to leave Jack's side, and she couldn't blame her. She felt her own tears forming as she looked at him lying there.

"I talked to your sister. She said that she and your parents are going to try to get the next flight out of Birmingham. She'll call me when she has the details."

"Thank you," Cheryl said, wiping her eyes. "Were you able to get hold of Katie?"

Norma hesitated. "Not yet. I think her cell phone must be turned off. I'll try her again in a little while." Cheryl was in no shape to learn of Katie's plight.

~

The tires on the car plowed through the wet highway, casting water on either side of them.

Katie saw they had been driving for almost an hour since the helicopter had flown over. She knew they were headed for the border.

The wipers made a steady thump as they went back and forth across the windshield. She heard a crinkling noise and turned to see her abductor reaching into his pocket for a cigarette. She studied him for a moment. He was wearing a light blue Hawaiian shirt and dark jeans that had a neat crease in them. His silver hair, which matched the color of his goatee, was pulled back into a ponytail. He looked just like any ordinary man you would see walking down the street.

He held the steering wheel between his knees as he lit the cigarette.

Katie's eyes suddenly grew wide. "How do you know my name?" she whispered.

"*What?*" he said, turning towards her. "Are you *surprised* that I know your name?" He cracked the window and held his cigarette near it. "You're Katie Winstead, owner, and operator of *Katie's Bakery* on Main Street. You live at 130 Fleming Drive...and you are the girlfriend of Chief Sommers."

She suppressed a shudder.

"I saw you last week at *The Sea Shack* with the chief. The two of you were holding hands and making eyes at each other. I've been watching you for a while now, Katie." He gave her a twisted smile. "You're sweet. Just like your chocolate chip cookies."

Katie felt her stomach turn over.

"You know the old adage, 'Keep your friends close, but your enemies closer'? Well, that deputy caught me by surprise, leaving me with no choice but to kill him." He took a long drag off his cigarette. "It wasn't very satisfying."

She watched as he exhaled the smoke from his lungs.

"After that, I figured I just might need some leverage." He reached over and ran the tip of his finger down her jawline.

She closed her eyes and tried not to flinch.

"You're my leverage."

Ping.

He looked down at the dashboard. "*Shit.*"

From where she was seated, Katie could see a flashing orange icon in the shape of a gas pump. She peered through the windshield as the wipers swept the rain off, trying to look for the next mile marker. She figured, at best, they could drive another thirty miles or so.

~

"Mattingly!" Nathan motioned for him to come over as he hopped out of his truck. He spread the map out on the hood of the car and clicked on his flashlight.

"Did you get something?"

"I just got off the phone with my deputy. He searched Bryant's home and found that he has some property in Saskatchewan near Big Muddy Lake."

Mattingly looked at the map. "That's about thirty miles northeast of Whitetail."

Nathan listened as the trooper radioed the information in. He asked that the helicopter search that area and then trace back towards the interstate.

When he was done, he gave him a nod. "We're close, Sommers. I can feel it."

Nathan recognized the look in his eyes. It was the thrill of the hunt. You could stay awake for days just on adrenaline alone. In his early years as a detective, he used to feel that same way. But this time was different. The troopers could have Bryant. He just wanted Katie safely in his arms.

~

Bryant pushed the car off the road and into the brush. He hurried to the passenger's side and yanked the door open. "Get out."

Katie's shoes immediately sank into the soft ground that had been saturated with rain.

Bryant tore off a long strip of duct tape and roughly applied it across her mouth. He grabbed her by the arm and held the knife to her. "You do exactly as I say and I might just let you live. Understand?"

She blinked back tears as she nodded.

"Let's go," he said, jerking on her arm.

They began walking at a fast pace through a cluster of trees. The terrain was rough, and mostly downhill, making it extremely difficult for her to keep her balance with her hands bound behind her.

~

Daylight was beginning to break as Nathan looked out at the horizon. The rain had diminished a little while ago, leaving the air around him damp and muggy. Leaning against his truck, he watched the steam rise up from the road like an eerie fog.

The sound of someone shouting made him turn around. Several troopers were getting in their cars and heading north.

"Sommers!" Mattingly was running towards him.

"What's going on?"

"The chopper just spotted the victim's car abandoned in some brush about ten miles from Whitetail."

Nathan scrambled for his truck.

Mattingly ran alongside him. "If he *is* headed towards his cabin, he's got a lot of territory to cover first. We're going to try and surround him."

~

Katie hit the ground hard, knocking the breath out of her.

Her captor grabbed her underneath her right arm and yanked her up. "Keep moving."

The woods were thick with overgrown bushes, and tall, thin tree trunks. As they wound their way through it, she thought at first that her eyes must have adapted to the darkness, but then she saw that it was beginning to get light.

Her captor gave her a rough tug, signaling her to stop. He looked to his left and then to his right before looking down. "*Shit!*"

Katie followed his gaze. They were standing on a precipice that dropped at least a hundred feet. She could see that it had a slight incline to it as it descended into the forest below.

The man pushed on Katie's shoulders forcing her to sit on the wet ground. He then reached out and grasped on to a small tree as he took a step down. He held onto the trunk with one hand and grabbed her left arm with his other.

He jerked her down with such force that she slammed into him, putting her face inches from his.

"*I* take a step and then *you* take a step," he said in a low voice. "Understand?"

Before she could nod, he had already moved on to the next tree. He yanked her towards him, though not as hard this time. He then advanced to the next tree and repeated his actions.

Katie blindly put one foot in front of the other as she stumbled after him. Her arm was throbbing from him pulling on it.

The unmistakable sound of a helicopter overhead made her look up, but the denseness of the trees prevented her from seeing anything other than branches.

He quickened his pace, dragging her along with him, as the ground began to level out.

Her face was cut and bleeding from the branches and briars that would slap back against her as they ran.

Up ahead, she suddenly heard voices and shouts, but before she could do anything at all, he had pulled her to her knees. Her captor's hand instantly closed around her windpipe as he squatted beside her.

At the top of the precipice, she could see several police officers moving east.

Her captor's grip around her throat grew tighter as he watched, making it impossible for her to draw a breath. She began to panic and pedaled backward in an attempt to get out of his grasp.

He released his grip and pulled her up, giving her no time to recover. They were on the move again.

~

Nathan and Mattingly had been traveling on foot for about an hour now. They were following well behind the others in hopes that they could encircle Bryant and flush him out.

Drops of sweat trickled down Nathan's face as he ran over the muddy terrain. A few feet ahead, he could see that the ground suddenly dropped off. He stopped at the edge and bent over to catch his breath. "I think they may have headed this way."

Mattingly caught up to him and looked down. "This runs into a gentle slope about five miles that way," he said, pointing east with his fingers. "That's probably how they went."

Both men turned and began to run along the edge of the embankment.

Mattingly had picked up speed and was now several yards ahead of him.

Something inside Nathan made him stop running. If Bryant had come this way, he may have gone down over the side, unaware that there was an easier way. He looked to his left. Mattingly had disappeared out of his sight.

Leaning down, he put his hands on the edge of the embankment and hoisted himself over. He half-slid, half-fell, and half-rolled down it, finally stopping when it leveled out. His eyes scanned the forest for any movement as his ears strained to hear anything.

~

Katie knelt on the ground behind the trunk of a large fallen tree. Her captor still held her by her arm, but they had not moved in a while. The cuts on her face stung from the sweat that was pouring out of her and she rolled her left shoulder upwards in an attempt to wipe her cheek on it. His fingers dug into her flesh, making her stop.

Her eyes darted about as she tried to get her bearings. An open field lay just beyond the trees to her left, and she could make out what appeared to be a barn, or farmhouse, about half a mile away. Subtly shifting her gaze, she saw that he was looking at it too.

He yanked her up to go, only to stop and crouch back down. He cocked his head to the side as if he were listening to something.

Katie listened as well, but couldn't hear anything over the pounding of her heart.

He suddenly ducked completely down and muttered something under his breath.

Her eyes grew wide as he reached into his pants and pulled out a gun.

Nathan's boots sank into the mud as he ran through the forest.

"Sommers? Do you copy?" Mattingly's voice came over his walkie-talkie.

He stopped to rest for a moment as he reached behind him for his radio. To the south, he noticed a farmhouse in the distance. "This is Sommers. Go ahead." He breathed hard as he waited for him to come back.

"What's your location?"

A loud crack suddenly rang out.

Nathan felt something whiz by his ear as the tree beside him splintered. The radio fell from his fingers as he scrambled to get behind the tree for cover.

"That's far enough, Chief!"

Nathan pressed his back against the trunk and peered over his shoulder as he drew his gun. He could see Bryant about thirty yards ahead crouching behind a log. Katie was nowhere to be seen.

His radio suddenly began to fill with chatter, as everyone wanted to know where the shot had come from. It lay in front of the tree, too far for him to reach.

"I want you to show yourself right now, Chief!"

He remained where he was.

"Sommers, you show yourself in the next ten seconds, or I *will* kill her!"

"How do I know you haven't already done that?" he yelled back.

Bryant fired a second shot in the same direction and then bent down to rip the tape off Katie's mouth. "Say something," he ordered, pressing the muzzle of the gun hard against her cheekbone.

Her breath quivered as she drew it in. "Nathan!"

Nathan involuntarily closed his eyes upon hearing her voice. She must be on the other side of the log with him.

"Did you hear that, Chief? She's all right. I want you to show yourself right now!"

Nathan glanced around, looking for a way to get behind them.

"Ten seconds, Nathan!" He dragged Katie out from behind the log, using her as a shield.

Nathan edged himself around the tree, letting Bryant see him.

Bryant took a step backward as he fastened his grip on Katie. "Walk slowly over here!"

He kept his gun trained on Bryant as he went towards them.

"That's far enough!"

Nathan stood directly in front of him now, about twenty feet away. He glanced at Katie. Her face was streaked with tears and blood. "It's going to be all right, Katie," he said, returning his eyes to Bryant.

She tried to answer him but the only thing she could manage was a sob.

"Let her go, Sam. You don't have a chance of getting out of here."

"Put your gun down!"

"You know I can't do that."

Bryant grabbed Katie by her hair and yanked it backward, eliciting a cry from her. "Don't think I won't put a bullet in her!"

Nathan's heart raced. "All right!" He lowered his gun and held it out to his side, his finger still on the trigger.

"Toss it!"

Nathan looked at Katie, his eyes locking with hers.

"Toss it!"

He threw it about ten feet in front of him. "You can't get away with this, Bryant! This place is going to be swarming with cops in about five minutes."

"You're the only one that knows where we are, Sommers."

"I can't let you take her with you," he said, trying to buy himself some time.

Bryant's voice suddenly became very calm. "Well, Nathan, you really don't have a choice. You see if I eliminate the threat, I eliminate the danger. And I still have a backup plan." He pointed his gun straight at him. *"You're* the threat, *she's* my backup plan." He pulled the trigger.

Nathan dropped to one knee and reached behind him for his other gun. A hard force tore through him as he aimed and fired.

Katie felt her captor's fingers slipping from her neck and then heard a loud thud. Trembling, she turned to look. Sam Bryant lay sprawled on the ground — unmoving and unblinking; a perfectly symmetrical hole now decorated the middle of his pale forehead.

"Katie…"

Spinning around, she saw Nathan coming towards her, his gun still on Bryant.

He suddenly stopped and sank to his knees.

"Nathan!" She could see a dark liquid seeping through his t-shirt as she ran towards him.

He fell backward as he fought to breathe. A moment later, he saw Katie's beautiful face leaning over him. She was shouting something at him, but he couldn't hear. He closed his eyes as he felt his breath leaving him.

Chapter Twenty-four

Katie sat alone in an interview room at the Scobey Police Department. For the last five hours, she had been asked countless times to go over her ordeal. She tucked a strand of hair behind her ear as she stared at the door. It seemed, at least for now, that they were satisfied with what she had told them.

She looked down at the billowing sweatshirt surrounding her. One of the officers had given it to her upon her arrival. The sleeves extended over her hands by at least six inches, but she didn't mind. It was warm and comfortable and hid the bandages on her wrists.

The wooden door swung open as Officer Dunn came back into the room. She recognized him as being one of the men that had first come to her aid.

He sat down in the chair next to her and slid three crisp papers in front of her. "Ms. Winstead, this is the statement that you've given us," he said in a gentle voice. "I'd like for you to read it over, and make sure that it's correct before signing it."

She looked at the pages as she pretended to read them. If they had made a mistake typing the information after she had repeated it twelve times, it was their own *damn* fault. Grasping the pen with her fingers, she hurriedly scrawled her name on the line and slid the papers back to him.

Dunn looked at her for a long time before speaking. "I wanted to let you know that I spoke with Deputy Hoskins a little while ago. He said to tell you that he fed your cat."

Her eyes began to sting as she nodded.

He gathered the papers and stood up. "If you'll wait here, I'll arrange for an officer to drive you back to Silver Creek."

Chapter Twenty-five

Katie stood solemnly in front of her bathroom mirror brushing her hair. For the past three days, everything she had done seemed like it had been in slow motion.

Her eyes caught sight of her wrists as she put the brush down. The redness was no longer there, but the cuts were still deep.

She slid open the top drawer of the vanity and pulled out her makeup. A liberal amount of concealer helped to cover the dark circles and puffiness under her eyes, while foundation and blush helped disguise the gauntness in her cheeks. Her appetite was close to non-existent, and sleep only brought unwanted nightmares of Sam Bryant. She saw him every time she closed her eyes.

When she was through, she looked at her reflection. She tugged on the sleeve of her dress, but it did nothing to help hide the upper part of her arms, which were mottled with dark-purple bruises.

Tired of the view, she clicked off the light and walked into her bedroom.

Lance lay sprawled out on her comforter as she sat down to slip on her shoes. He yawned and began to purr as she rubbed him on his head. He had stayed close to her since her return, rarely leaving her side.

Glancing at the clock on the nightstand, she realized Norma would soon be here to pick her up. Her car was still impounded by the Scobey City Police. When she would get it back was anybody's guess.

She patted Lance on his head and grabbed her black cardigan. It would be too hot to wear, but at least it would cover up her arms and wrists.

Reaching over, she unplugged her cell from its charger and started to slip it into her purse. It was then that she noticed she had a voice mail waiting. The only thing she had done with her phone since returning home was charge it, as she hadn't felt like talking to anyone. She pressed the button with her thumb and waited.

"Katie, it's Nathan."

Her heart leaped into her throat as she gripped the phone with both hands.

"I got your message that you left for me earlier tonight." There was a long pause, followed by the sound of him taking a trembling breath. "I can't begin to imagine what you're going through right now, but I swear to God I'm going to get you back safe. I wish I could talk to you and hear your sweet voice."

Her eyes began to fill with tears as she listened to him go on.

"When this is all over, I want to hold you in my arms, and never let you go."

Chapter Twenty-six

The funeral procession was long. The cars were lined up at least a half-mile behind the hearse as it slowly made its way down the street.

Katie and Cheryl held hands, silently leaning on one another for support.

As they turned into St. Mary's Cemetery, Katie saw the sun beginning to break through the clouds. She looked out the darkened window of the limo and noticed all the statues of the saints that lined the entrance. They were supposed to evoke comfort, but she found each one to be more morose than the next.

The limo rolled to a stop and the driver came around, helping her and Cheryl out.

As they made their way over to the chairs, Katie heard car door after car door open and shut behind her. They sat down in the front row as throngs of people filed past them. It seemed that most of the town had turned out today to bury their fallen.

Katie glanced at her friend. Her arm was resting lightly on her stomach as tears streamed down her face. Cheryl's sister, along with her parents, sat quietly on the other side of her. She squeezed her hand, knowing that they were going to need each other more than ever for the dark days that lay ahead.

The doors of the hearse opened and three men she had never seen before got out and walked around to the back of it.

A moment later, Mayor Manning, Si, and Jack appeared on the other side. They slowly began to slide the casket out on the steel rollers.

A cry fell from Katie's lips as they prepared to lift it.

Cheryl saw the grimace on Jack's face as he hoisted the casket upon his shoulders. The doctor had released him from the hospital this morning so he could attend the funeral.

Forty-eight hours ago, she remembered thanking God for answering her prayers as her husband had finally opened his eyes. Her elation was short-lived, however, as four hours after that, Norma tearfully told her everything that had happened.

She watched as they carried the casket over to the grave and stopped. In one swift motion, they set it down on the metal straps and stepped back.

Jack stood alongside Hoskins in full dress uniform, the tears falling freely down the side of his face. Having to tell him about Nathan was the hardest thing she had ever done. He had been inconsolable.

The mayor stood behind the small wooden podium for several moments without speaking.

For the first time Cheryl could ever recall, Tom Manning was at a loss for words.

Finally, he looked out across the townsfolk and cleared his throat. "We are gathered here today to pay tribute to Chief of Police Nathan Sommers, who bravely gave his life in the line of duty." He drew an unsteady breath. "As a policeman, Nathan was aware of the inherent risks of wearing the badge, and in the early hours of July fifth, he saved the life of a young woman without giving any thought to his own."

Cheryl put her hands over her mouth trying to suppress the sobs. She closed her eyes as a flood of tears came. Exactly nine days ago, they had stood in the kitchen celebrating Nathan's birthday. It was the last time they were all together.

She held onto Katie's hand tightly. Nothing that ever was, would be the same again.

Manning continued on. "Nathan and I didn't always see eye to eye...I guess because as a father, I never felt anyone could be good enough for my little girl—" His voice suddenly broke. He stopped and shook his head slightly. "But I was very proud to have called him my son-in-law."

Katie wiped at her eyes but couldn't stop the tears from coming. She felt as if she had been laid bare, split open from head to toe. She drowned out the mayor's voice, replacing it with Nathan's. Her mind replayed the message over and over, committing his words to memory. She heard every breath he took and every inflection in his voice.

She didn't regret the time that she had spent at Silver Creek, or what had happened to her. And although deep down she loved Nathan, she knew he was in a better place. He was finally at peace.

Nathan was buried that day with full honors and was laid to rest beside Jenny.

No family members ever stepped forward to claim the body of Sam Bryant. He was buried in an unmarked grave.

~~~

Thank you for taking the time to read *The Monster of Silver Creek*. If you enjoyed it, please consider telling your friends or posting a short review. Word of mouth is an author's best friend and very much appreciated.

~ Thank you, Belinda G. Buchanan

And now, I'd like to invite you to learn more about the characters in the sequel, *Tragedy at Silver Creek.*

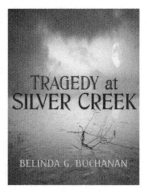

Guilt is a very powerful thing, and Deputy Jack Collins is mired in it. Unable to forget the events that have taken place in the town he was sworn to protect, he feels as if he is slowly drowning as he tries to adjust to fatherhood, as well as his new — and unwanted — job as chief of police.

When the body of a young woman, having the same puncture wounds as the serial killer's previous victims, is discovered, Jack must determine if this is a copycat crime or the work of a possible accomplice — either of which — could put the killer's only surviving victim in grave danger.

WINTER'S MALICE

In Weeping Rock, South Dakota—a small town crippled by racism, drugs, and violence—Sheriff's Deputy Liam Matthews has his work cut out for him when he steps in to take over the duties of sheriff from his father, who for far too long has turned a blind eye to certain crimes for what he says is the overall good of the town.

Coming under scrutiny for hiring a Lakota to fill his position as deputy, things quickly go from bad to worse for Liam when the body of retired pro-baseball player Hector Ramirez, who had recently returned home to coach ball at his high school alma mater, is found floating in Crow's Foot Lake. Hector's bludgeoned corpse is no sooner on its way to the M.E.'s office in Rapid City, however, when the partially clothed body of a young girl is discovered in a clearing in the snow.

With two seemingly unrelated murders, Liam is judged at every turn of his investigation by the local population, Hector's reality TV star wife Kiki Grey, and his own father. Upon uncovering a tangled web of desperation, lies, and greed, the mounting pressure inside Liam to do the right thing becomes jaded when the skeletal remains of a third victim is found in a submerged car, bringing to the forefront a long-buried secret of his own — and threatening his already troubled marriage to Olivia — as his past and present collide.

AFTER ALL IS SAID AND DONE

At thirty-four years of age, Ethan Harrington is a brilliant doctor, devoted husband, eager father to be—and borderline alcoholic. He has spent the better part of a year trying to forgive his wife, Jessica, for her infidelity, but her betrayal with a colleague of his has left him hurt beyond words.

That hurt slowly begins to heal with the birth of his son, but it isn't long before he learns the devastating secret that Jessica has been trying to keep from him. Ethan's life steadily begins to crumble—and his drinking, fueled by this discovery, slowly engulfs him.

With his marriage now in pieces and his sanity questionable, Ethan struggles to come to terms with his alcoholism and face a past that he has spent a lifetime trying to forget.

SEASONS OF DARKNESS

Long before Ethan Harrington's turbulent marriage to Jessica, he was just a lonely young man trying to cope with his mother's suicide.

Left alone with his controlling father in an isolated farmhouse, he struggles to live among the shattered remains of a family that was never functional to begin with.

A kindhearted doctor, a beautiful girl, and a caring nanny all love him in different ways, but Ethan, still ravaged by his mother's death, turns to what he has seen his father take comfort in time and time again—thus giving rise to an inner demon that will not turn him loose.

About the author

I write edgy, Women's Fiction and Mystery novels. The characters that I write about are not perfect. They are far from it, actually. Even heroes have a chink in their armor. It's what makes them human.

My stories are filled with emotion, intimacy, drama, and hope. If you like these things and don't mind a few racy scenes, or a sprinkling of profanity here and there, then my books are for you.

Late at night, you'll find me holed up in my office/closet gleefully typing away on my keyboard. It's a place where tall, dark, and handsome meets high drama — and is located just underneath the winter coats.

Hailing from the bluegrass state, I still live there with my husband of twenty-nine years, my two sons: one who loves me unconditionally, and one who only loves me when we're not in public. I am a professional hamster wrangler, lover of cats, and a firm believer that Krazy Glue fixes everything.

To find out more about my novels and myself, you can visit my **Website:**
belindagbuchanan.com

I love to talk almost as much as I love to write, so come chat with me on **Facebook:**
www.facebook.com/Belinda.G.Buchanan.author

Or **Twitter**: twitter.com/BelindaBuchanan

And if you're a pinner, come find me on **Pinterest**:
http://www.pinterest.com/belindabuchanan

Made in United States
Orlando, FL
18 May 2023

33240013R00173